PLAYING WITH FIRE . . .

Maybe he's never met the right girl before, Laura told herself. *Maybe I'm the right girl for him. And he's the right guy for me . . .*

Laura rubbed her shoulder anxiously. *I shouldn't be thinking about him this way,* she reminded herself. *I don't want a player like Mark.*

"Do you want me to do that?" Mark asked. "My mom taught me a good technique for relaxing muscles."

Laura froze. Did she want him to touch her? More than she would ever admit. But could she actually *let* him? *It's just a little massage,* she rationalized. "Yeah, sure," she responded, trying her hardest to sound nonchalant.

Mark came over and started to massage her neck and shoulders. Laura leaned against him, relaxed and at the same time more alert than she'd ever been in her life.

"Is this better?" he said softly into her ear.

"Yes," she whispered.

Slowly he turned her toward him, and they faced each other, inches apart.

Laura's breath caught, and the whole room seemed suspended in time. She looked into his eyes, her heart thumping a million beats a minute.

And then he pressed his lips against hers. Laura let herself melt into the kiss, and it was . . . incredible. Explosive. She put her arms around Mark, holding him and shutting out everything but the delicious sensation of his mouth on hers.

Love Stories

Stolen Kisses

LIESA ABRAMS

BANTAM BOOKS
NEW YORK · TORONTO · LONDON · SYDNEY · AUCKLAND

RL 6, age 12 and up

STOLEN KISSES

A Bantam Book / June 1999

Cover photography by Michael Segal.

 Produced by 17th Street Productions,
a division of Daniel Weiss Associates, Inc.
33 West 17th Street, New York, NY 10011.

ISBN: 0-553-49288-8

Published simultaneously in the United States and Canada

PRINTED IN THE UNITED STATES OF AMERICA

OPM   0 9 8 7 6 5 4 3 2 1

To Sean, for helping me believe in happy endings, and to my mother, for making mine possible.

ONE

LAURA WHITMAN GAZED around the school auditorium in amazement. Everything looked exactly the same as it had when she'd taken her final curtain call last June: rows of slightly dusty seats, lighting equipment stacked in the corner, discarded scenery leaning against the back wall of the stage. But now, somehow, it all seemed different. Sliding into a seat near the front, Laura turned her focus to the stage, its scratched wooden floor gleaming in the overhead lights. She smiled as she pictured herself up there in full costume, delivering her monologues as Samantha, the star of the play *Only Today.*

I'm really going to do it, she thought in astonishment. *I'm really the lead actress!* Excitement washed over her as she remembered seeing her name at the top of the cast list when it had been posted last spring, at the end of her sophomore year. All summer she'd been waiting for this

1

moment: her first rehearsal as the female lead.

"Hey, Laura!"

She turned to see Stacey Muzin and Amanda London, two other drama club members. "Hi, Stace, Amanda. How've you guys been?"

Stacey flipped her long, blond hair behind her shoulder. "I can't say I'm thrilled to be back in school, but at least the play should be fun."

"Of course, we can't all have leads like you, Laura," Amanda added.

Laura and Amanda were two of the most talented actresses at Park Hills High—and as a result had always been up for the same roles in the plays. The unspoken rivalry between them had heated up now that Emily Griffin, star of the show for the past two years, had graduated. Laura couldn't help being psyched about snagging the lead over Amanda.

"Remember what Ms. Goldstein says," Laura told Amanda. "There are no small parts, only—"

"Small actors, we know," Stacey finished, laughing. "She loves to use that line on me, since I'm always playing totally unimportant characters who are,"—she paused and struck the pose their drama teacher always took before lectures—"absolutely quintessential to the play."

Laura laughed. Even if Stacey always got small roles, she was great at imitating other people.

"It's really filling up," Amanda commented, glancing around the auditorium. "Hey! There's Jordan Wallens. Look how hot he got over the summer!"

Stacey rolled her eyes. "I guess we're gonna go

socialize some more," she joked as Amanda tugged on her sleeve. "See you later."

"See ya," Laura said. She watched them walk over to where Jordan was sitting, then turned back to face the stage. She tuned out the chattering voices around her, returning to her daydream about opening night. The curtains would open, and she would be up there alone. The cast and crew would be counting on her to make the production a success. *Well, not just me,* she thought. *Me and—*

The sound of someone sitting down next to her pulled her out of her fantasy. Laura turned—and her heart jumped into her throat.

Oh my God. It can't be. He wouldn't—not next to me.

"Hi, Laura, what's up?" Ted Legum grinned at her, his light gray eyes filled with friendly warmth, his blond hair perfectly tousled.

Wait a minute, she thought. Ted Legum, the most gorgeous senior at Park Hills High, who'd been getting leading roles since he was a sophomore, was actually talking to *her? Okay, universe, check your alignment, quickly.* He was still looking at her! Maybe he expected her to answer him or something normal like that. What was the matter with her?

"Ted, hi. I'm fine. Great. I mean, nothing much. Nothing much is up, I mean." *I pulled that off pretty well, right? Especially if my objective was to make sure he never talks to me again,* she thought, mentally kicking herself.

Ted laughed. "I see you're feeling the effects of being back in school too. It's hard to deal with the end of summer."

"Oh, yeah. Definitely," Laura managed. The effects of being back in school? Try the effects of being spoken to by the most unattainable guy at Park Hills. Not only was Ted good-looking and popular, but he'd been going out with Emily Griffin ever since they played Tony and Maria in *West Side Story* two years ago. *I wonder if he's still with Emily now that she's at college,* Laura thought.

Ted stretched out his arms, his green polo shirt emphasizing his lean upper body. Laura looked down at her own outfit in a sudden fit of panic. Navy capri pants with a white V-necked shirt. Did she look okay? If she'd known Ted would choose today to sit with her as if they were old friends, she certainly would have picked out her clothes much more carefully.

"So, you excited about the play?" Ted asked her.

Laura gulped, feeling her pulse speed up. Was Ted worried about playing opposite her? Did he think she would be awful compared to Emily?

"I, um, I guess so." She ran her fingers through her brown curls and tried to avoid twisting the ends around her finger like she always did when she was nervous. Her best friend, Rosita Manolo, had warned her that it made her look young. "I'm glad it's not a musical this year. I can't sing. I mean, not like Emily. I mean . . ." Laura's voice trailed off. Had she just made a total fool of herself?

Ted flicked a piece of dust off his legs, straightening

out his khaki pants at the same time. "Yeah, well, not many people can sing like Em."

Laura looked at him sympathetically. He must really miss his girlfriend. "So, how is Emily? Does she like college so far?"

Ted shrugged. "I don't really know. We decided to break up before she went away—we figured a long-distance relationship would be too hard to pull off."

Laura bit her lip. *Great job*, she told herself, *bringing up his ex the minute he gets back to school.*

"I'm sorry," she said lamely

Ted grinned at her. "It's okay. It was time we got to know other people anyway."

Laura blinked in surprise as Ted gazed into her eyes. "Hey, by the way," he started. "Have you seen *Way of the Road*? I heard it's pretty good."

"Uh, no. Have you?" Laura winced. "Well, no, obviously you haven't. . . ." Somehow she couldn't find the right words with him looking at her like that.

"Do you want to see it this weekend? If you don't have other plans, that is."

Laura stared at him blankly, trying to absorb the fact that Ted had just asked her out. Other plans? Gee, should she cancel her date to do nothing by herself in order to go out with a gorgeous senior?

"I'm pretty open," she said. "That would be great." Laura took a deep breath, congratulating herself on making her first coherent remark in the whole conversation.

"Okay. How's Saturday night?"

"Saturday's perfect," she declared.

"Cool."

Laura sat back in her seat, her mind reeling. She and Ted Legum had a *date!* As in, an evening together, just the two of them, that would probably lead to a kiss at the end and possibly to further evenings with more kisses.

Would it look strange if I leaped out of my seat and started singing at the top of my lungs while doing cartwheels around the theater? Laura wondered, closing her eyes in bliss.

Just then the voices in the auditorium quieted down. Laura knew this meant that their director must have arrived, but she was too caught up with her fantasies about Saturday to focus on the present.

"Hey, what's Adams doing here?" Ted asked.

Laura's eyes popped open. "Mark Adams?" she asked.

Ted gestured toward the stage, and Laura saw Mark following her drama teacher onto the stage. As usual, Laura felt a rush of attraction toward Mark. And as usual, she forced the thoughts out of her mind.

"I don't know," Laura responded. "I've never seen him act before. Except when he's hitting on some innocent girl."

Ted raised his eyebrows. "How does he act then?"

"Oh, he just acts like he's completely in love with her until she goes out with him. Then he acts like he has no idea why she expects anything from him."

Ted laughed. "I take it you're not fond of him?"

6

Suddenly Laura realized how she must sound to Ted. "Oh, I'm not talking about myself!" she cried. "I would never go out with a guy like that—he's a total player. But my friend Rosita is friends with Mark. I hear about all his girls from her."

She watched Mark shake his long, dark hair out of his face. There were a lot of guys as cute as him—Ted, for instance. But unlike Mark, Ted was a good guy. Everyone knew how well he had treated Emily. So what if Mark was good-looking? It always amazed her that girls continued to fall for Mark even though they knew he was a jerk. Laura had never been able to understand why Rosita put up with him.

"Okay, everyone, settle down." Ms. Goldstein pulled two chairs to the front of the stage and sat down in one, motioning for Mark to sit in the other. "This is Mark Adams. He's going to be my assistant director for the fall play."

Laura frowned in annoyance. Mark would probably date half the cast before the show even started. With him around, the play wouldn't be as much fun as she had expected. Unless . . . She stole a quick glance at Ted. Maybe their date this weekend would lead to something more. If she ended up being Ted's girlfriend, then this play would be the most absolutely and completely perfect experience of her life. She took a deep breath to slow down her heartbeat and tried to focus on what the drama teacher was saying.

"I know this is a little unusual," Ms. Goldstein

continued, "but Mark came to me with the idea, and I thought it would be great to involve students in all aspects of the production. I'll still be running things, but you should listen to all of Mark's comments and directions as if they were coming from me." She stopped, clearing her throat. "Now, let's get started. I'd like to begin with a reading of the script, so if you could all get yours out. . . ."

Laura bent down to unzip her backpack, pulling out her copy of *Only Today*. Opening it to the first page, Laura sank back in her seat, still trying desperately not to pass out from sheer excitement. Between the play and her date with Ted, this year was starting out great.

"Okay, let me get this straight. He just sat down next to you, like it was the most normal thing in the world, and within minutes you scored yourself a date?"

Laura laughed as she tried to untwist the phone cord. "Thanks for the vote of confidence, Rosi." She finally pulled out the last kink, then stretched the receiver over to the fridge so that she could look for something to drink.

"Well, no offense, but it isn't every day that you get asked out by really hot seniors, you know," Rosita replied.

Laura barely heard her friend's comment. She was too busy searching the top shelf. "Darn," she muttered.

"Oh, so now it's a problem?" Rosita asked in an amused tone.

"No." Laura sighed. "Julie must've finished the orange juice."

"Okay, let's see. . . . On a scale of importance, which rates higher, your sister drinking all the juice or your date with Ted Legum?" Rosita paused.

Laura giggled, closing the refrigerator door and plopping down on a chair at the kitchen table. "I know, I know," she said. "God, I never imagined I'd be telling you that Ted and I have a *date*." For the millionth time that day Laura felt her heart thump wildly.

"Dennis will be happy when he hears the news. You know how he's always complaining about the ratio of estrogen to testosterone when we hang out."

Laura smiled. Dennis was Rosita's boyfriend, and they'd been together for what seemed like forever. Laura knew Rosita was only teasing—Dennis had always been a good sport when it came to their three-person outings.

"Come on, like he doesn't get a kick out of walking around with two stunning babes all the time," Laura kidded back.

"Speak for yourself," Rosita commented.

Laura shook her head—Rosita always criticized her own looks, somehow failing to recognize how beautiful her classic Filipino features were.

"Okay, Rosi, here's the deal," Laura said, getting up to look in the cabinet above the sink for a snack. "Your resolution for junior year is to stop being so down on yourself. You're beautiful, your boyfriend adores you, and you have everything going for you." She spotted a box of crackers.

"Sorry if I don't subscribe to the Laura Whitman school of thought," Rosita responded. "But the world isn't actually as flawlessly perfect as you think it is."

Laura grabbed the crackers and sat back down. "I don't think the world is *completely* without flaws," she joked. "These crackers would be better with orange juice."

Rosita snorted.

"Anyway, why are we talking about this?" Laura went on. "What we should be discussing is how to make sure I don't mess this Ted thing up."

"How would you mess it up?" Rosita asked.

"Well, for starters, I sounded like an idiot talking to him today." She felt herself redden as she remembered their conversation. But when she thought of his light gray eyes, she immediately cheered up.

"This is so cute," Rosita said, giggling. "You really like him, don't you?"

Laura thought about it for a second. Ted was an amazing actor, and he seemed so mature and sophisticated. "Yeah, I guess I do," she answered.

"You do what?" Laura's sister, Julie, asked from the kitchen doorway.

"I'll tell you later, Jules. Did you finish that?" Laura pointed to the orange juice container in Julie's hand.

"Yeah, sorry." Julie walked by her and threw it in the trash can. Her usually bright green eyes looked dull.

"Hold on a sec," Laura said into the phone.

Then she turned to her sister. "What's wrong?"

Julie looked back at her blankly. "Nothing." She started to walk away.

"Wait—" Laura rested the phone on her shoulder.

But Julie pushed past her and quickly walked out of the kitchen.

Laura scooped the receiver back up. "Sorry about that. I'm kind of worried about Julie. She's been acting weird lately."

"How so?" Rosita asked.

"I don't know—just not like herself. Usually we tell each other everything. But it seems like she's holding out on me or something. Maybe I'm just overreacting."

"Probably," Rosita agreed. "I'm sure it's nothing major. I mean, the girl is twelve. We all went through periods of weirdness back then."

Laura nodded—Rosita was right. Julie was most likely just suffering from prepubescent angst. "That's true."

"Oh, before I forget," Rosita went on. "There's a party at this guy Raphael Zinman's house on Friday night. Dennis knows him, so we're gonna go. You in?"

"Sure. And who knows, maybe my date on Saturday will go so well that I'll never have to do the threesome thing with you and Dennis again," Laura said.

Rosita laughed. "Yeah, think positive. And a lot of people are going. I told Sara about it, and Berna and Erica and Mark."

"Mark Adams?" Laura paused, trying to make sure her voice sounded normal. "How come?" Even though Rosita and Mark were friends, they didn't socialize much outside of school. Which was just how Laura liked it—if Rosi didn't hang out with Mark, that meant Laura didn't have to hang out with him either. She'd never had the courage to tell her best friend that she'd had a major crush on Mark last year. Of course, that was *before* Rosita told her about how badly Mark treated the girls he went out with. Now Laura just wanted to stay as far away from him as possible.

"It's a giant back-to-school-bash kind of thing. I thought it would be nice to see all my friends at once for a change," Rosita explained. "But actually, if Mark does come, I probably won't see much of him. He'll be too busy hitting on innocent freshmen!"

"Ugh, how can he use girls like that?" Laura asked, crinkling her nose in disgust. "Doesn't he feel bad at all? Doesn't he want something more genuine?"

"I don't know," Rosita said. "I try to ignore the big-flirt part of his personality. But he *is* a decent guy once you get to know him. I don't know why you hate him so much."

Because it's the only way I can keep from liking *him,* Laura thought.

She heard the sound of a car outside. "I think my mom just pulled up. I'm dying to tell her about Ted. Call you later, okay?"

"Sure. Bye, Laura."

"Bye."

"Girls, I'm home!" her mom called out from the foyer.

Laura smiled. Her mother always announced her arrival in the same cheery voice. "Hi, Mom!" she yelled back.

"How was rehearsal, sweetie?" her mom asked as she walked into the kitchen.

"Amazing. You are not going to believe this," Laura said, bouncing up and down on her heels and beaming at her mother.

"Let's see." Mrs. Whitman sat down and motioned for Laura to sit across from her. "Ms. Goldstein told you the play's going to be on Broadway instead of in Park Hills?" Her brown eyes sparkled.

"Nope." Laura paused, wanting to make the most of the moment. "Okay, get this. Ted Legum asked *me* to go out with him this weekend! He broke up with Emily, and now we're going out on Saturday night!" The words spilled out of her mouth at warp speed.

"Ted? Your costar in the play?"

"Yes! Isn't it too incredible?" She jumped up, unable to sit still for a moment longer.

Her mom reached out and squeezed her arm. "Well, I hope this boy deserves you."

"Mom, this boy is absolutely *perfect* for me," Laura promised. "In fact, right now my entire life is absolutely perfect!"

TWO

"WHERE ARE THOSE stupid keys?" Mark muttered, searching through the mess on the coffee table. He wondered if maybe this was a sign that he shouldn't go to the party. He wasn't really into it anyway.

He heard the sound of the lock turning in the front door and turned just as his mother walked into their apartment. "Hey, Mom," he greeted her.

"Hi." She immediately sank into the sofa, rubbing her temples with her fingers. His mom was a social worker and worked long hours at a hospital in southern New Jersey. Every evening when she came home, she would follow the same pattern. Mark knew she'd be asleep within the hour, even though it was only eight on a Friday night.

Of course, right now the idea of sleep appealed to him too. Mark never functioned well in big social situations, and he wasn't sure what it would be like to hang out with Rosita's friends at a party. He figured it could be okay, as long as her friend Abby wasn't there. She had become way too clingy after their one stupid kiss in the cafeteria last year.

"Are you going out with Mike and Doug?" his mom asked, looking up at him.

"No, not tonight." Mark's Friday nights were usually as predictable as his mother's—he'd either be at Mike's house, hanging with him and Doug, or he'd be out with some girl. But tonight Mike and Doug were at a Yankees game in the city—baseball, in Mark's opinion, was second only to golf as the most boring spectator sport—and Mark hadn't met any new girls recently.

"Rosita wants me to go to some party," he continued without much enthusiasm. "I guess it'll be okay. I can't find my car keys, though." Mark resumed his scan of the living room. He treasured the used Nissan Sentra that he'd bought with money from work and holiday gifts. Normally the keys were never far from his sight.

"You don't sound like you're dying to go." His mother adjusted her legs, and Mark noticed how she winced at the movement. Ever since a car accident she'd been in before he was born, his mom had lived with chronic back pain. He hated seeing those expressions on her face, knowing that each time she was fighting not to reveal just how much it really hurt.

"Mom, you look like you've had a rough day. Why don't you go lie down?"

She smiled at him. "I will. Are you going to the party?"

He shrugged. "Rosi really wants me to go, and she said—" He stopped, cutting himself off. *Mom doesn't need to know that Rosi mentioned there would be a lot of freshmen there,* he told himself. His mother wouldn't think scoping out new girls was a good reason for going. "Um, she said she'd be mad if I didn't go," he finished.

"Well, try to have a good time, then," she told him, yawning.

"Okay." Mark walked into his bedroom, shaking his head in anger. Sure, his job at the video store brought in extra cash, but not nearly enough to make a dent in their expenses.

Mark wondered what his father was doing at that precise moment. Was he happy? Relaxed? At peace? No, he was miserable, lonely, and racked with guilt over having left his wife and son years ago. It was a little game Mark always played, imagining where his dad was and then twisting the picture so that his so-called father was actually worse off than he and his mom were.

The minute Mark walked into his room, he spotted the car keys on top of the Beastie Boys CD he was planning to bring to the party. He chuckled to himself—he'd put them there so he'd be sure to remember the CD and then totally forgotten about it. *Typical me,* he thought.

He snatched up the keys and the disc before he had a chance to change his mind about going to the party.

"Don't stay out too late," his mother said as he hurried through the living room.

"I won't," he told her, giving her a kiss on her cheek. "Good night, Mom."

"Good night."

Mark paused in the hallway outside their apartment. He glanced down at the car keys.

How bad can one party be? he thought. *After all, maybe I'll meet a girl. Or two.*

Mark knocked a few times on the Zinmans' front door. While he waited to be let in, he took in the surroundings with awe. There were some beautiful, opulent houses in Upper Montclair, New Jersey. *Too bad they're all on the opposite end of town from where I live,* he thought wryly.

"Hey, man, come in." Mark regarded the guy who held open the front door to this mansion. He seemed vaguely familiar, probably someone Mark had seen once or twice in the hallways at Park Hills. "Help yourself to whatever you want." The guy turned and walked away, leaving Mark in the entryway.

Mark stood there for a second, looking around. The living room was big and airy, like something out of those home-decorating magazines he'd seen at his grandmother's house. The furniture was arranged at precise angles, and the paintings on the walls looked expensive yet tacky. Right now, the austere decor was offset by the noise of all the people there—along with the blaring music. Mark searched the crowd until he spotted Rosita and Dennis in the next room, then walked over to them.

"Mark!" Rosita exclaimed. "You made it!" She grinned at him. "Was it the prospect of my company that brought you out, or did you just come to meet—how can I put this—available girls?"

"I don't know what you mean," he said, trying to sound innocent.

Rosita and Dennis exchanged glances. "He came to meet girls," they said at the same time.

"You two are scary," came a voice from behind Mark. He turned to see Rosi's best friend, Laura Whitman. He caught her eye for a moment, then she quickly glanced away.

Mark didn't know Laura very well, but what he'd seen of her had confirmed every doubt he had about socializing with Rosita's friends. Rosi might be smart, funny, and a great writer, but she hung out with people like Laura—transparent types who you just knew spelled everything out on the surface: cushy life, perfect family, no questions or problems.

Still, Laura sure was beautiful. She looked even better tonight than he'd ever seen her, in a tight little skirt revealing endlessly long and shapely legs. Mark shook his head, forcing himself to push away thoughts of Laura's limbs. Instead he focused on trying to come up with some sort of polite and maybe slightly funny greeting.

"Hey, Laura, how's life?" he asked her. Well, the polite part worked at least.

"Good," she responded, studying him as if he were some strange chemistry experiment.

Rosita seemed to notice because she gave her friend a puzzled look. "So, should we mingle?" she asked cheerily.

Dennis groaned. "My girlfriend, the social butterfly, has felt the call of her species."

Mark smiled in sympathy. "Yep, we're in for it now." He glanced around, taking in the crowd. A couple of cute girls he didn't recognize were standing by the doorway of the massive kitchen. "I wouldn't mind making my way to the kitchen." He winked at Rosita, and she shook her head.

"Sounds like a plan," Dennis agreed.

They walked into the kitchen, and on the way Mark smiled at the girls he'd noticed. He saw one blush—the shorter one with red hair. He made a mental note to find his way back to her later on in the evening.

"Look at this spread," Rosita marveled. She stood in front of a large oak table full of every snack food known to man, as well as a wide array of beverages. She grabbed some nachos and started to munch.

"Wait a second. If you eat these, does that mean tomorrow I'll have to listen to you moan about how many calories you ingested tonight?" Laura asked Rosita. As she spoke, she reached out to take some pretzels herself, and Mark couldn't help but notice how tiny and delicate her hand was.

Okay, Adams, he told himself sternly. *Stop checking this girl out. She's Rosi's best friend, which makes her totally off-limits. Besides, you wouldn't be able to take her "life-is-perfect" attitude anyway.*

"I take the fifth on that one," Rosita answered, talking with a mouth full of food.

"What is it with you girls and your diets?" Mark asked.

"For your information," Laura said, "we worry about our weight because society judges us on every little aspect of our figures."

Mark really wished she hadn't said that—he was trying hard enough not to think about her figure right now.

"That's an overused excuse," he said. "All those women's magazines tell you that guys care about those things, so you rush out and—" He stopped abruptly, noticing that Dara Small had just walked into the kitchen. She was someone he did *not* want to see. How long had it taken for her to stop calling him after their one date?

"Uh, let's go back to the party, guys," he said hurriedly. "We should be socializing, right?" He started out of the room, angling himself between Rosita and Laura to hide from Dara's view. He noticed that Laura had that funny look on her face

21

again, as if she suspected him of doing something he wouldn't even know *how* to do.

Back in the living room, they squeezed themselves into the empty spaces on a plush leather sofa. Mark couldn't help wondering how much the Zinmans had paid for it. How many months of rent could his mom have afforded with the money these people shelled out for one couch?

A couple of Rosita's other friends came over to talk for a few minutes, girls Mark had met a couple of times and wasn't particularly impressed with. Sara Lasker—*too* cute. Erica Spiegel—kind of boring. Bernadette So—a little snotty. But they didn't stay long, and soon Mark, Laura, Rosita, and Dennis were alone together again.

"I hate this music," Laura moaned. "Who's controlling the CD player here?" She twisted around to look.

"What's wrong with this song?" Mark asked her.

Laura turned back to face him, frowning. "You like this?" She raised her eyebrows in obvious disagreement. "It's just so . . ." She trailed off, rotating her hands in what looked like an attempt to conjure up the end of her sentence. "It's melancholy," she finally pronounced with a look of triumph on her face.

"Yeah," Mark acknowledged. "So? What's the matter with that?"

Rosita sighed. "God, Mark, we're at a party. Shouldn't they be playing something more upbeat?" She smiled at Laura. "You'll have to forgive my socially challenged friend. He doesn't get the concept of lighthearted fun."

Mark gulped down the rest of his soda, then put the can on the floor. "A good song is a good song. If you can't stay mirthful just because of the background noise, then—"

"Mirthful?" Rosita burst out laughing. "What kind of word is that?"

"We can't take you anywhere," Dennis teased.

"Come on," Mark said lightly. "You know you love the controversy I bring to every occasion."

"Besides, music is more than just background noise," Laura put in, as if she hadn't heard Rosi and Dennis. "It's what sets the mood for the whole party. And since parties are supposed to be fun, the music should help *make* it fun."

Mark stared at her, surprised. She was actually *arguing* with him! Usually girls agreed with anything he said, or they giggled, or they just looked confused. Well, except for Rosita. She mostly rolled her eyes.

"The problem is that 'fun' music is usually *bad* music," he told her. "It's shallow."

Laura's cheeks flushed. "Just because something is upbeat doesn't mean it's shallow," she insisted. "Things can be deep and happy at the same time."

"Give me one example," he challenged her.

"That's enough!" Rosita interrupted. "If you guys are going to spend the whole night fighting over the stupid music, none of us will have fun."

Mark chuckled. "Okay, okay. Truce." He glanced

at Laura. She had a soft smile on her lips and was shaking her head slightly. This time when he caught her eye, she didn't turn away. She stared right back at him.

"What are *you* doing here?" asked a cold voice from behind him. He looked up, saw Dara Small, and winced. So she'd noticed him after all.

"Hey, Dara," he said.

"Don't you try to be friendly to me, you jerk!" she snapped. "You were supposed to meet me at the carnival, and you never showed up. Do you know how stupid I looked, standing there all alone?"

Mark groaned. "Dara, that was over a month ago—"

"Yeah, and you never even bothered to call and apologize!" she cut in. She raised her eyes to his friends. "I don't know how you can stand to hang out with him," she said. Then she turned and stormed away.

There was an awkward silence. "So what were we talking about?" Mark asked lamely.

Rosita frowned in mock disappointment. "We really *can't* take you anywhere."

Mark knew Rosi was only kidding, but her friend Laura must think he was some kind of monster. It wasn't his fault his car broke down on the way to meet Dara, although it sure was a good excuse to get out of their stupid carnival date.

He risked another look at Laura. Her smile had turned into a disapproving frown. To his dismay, her gaze shifted to someone near the stereo. "Hi,

24

Stacey," Laura called, waving enthusiastically.

A girl with a wide smile who Mark recognized from play rehearsal walked over. "Hey, Laura, I didn't know you'd be here." Her smile didn't shrink at all as she spoke. How did girls do that?

"Yeah, I came with Rosi."

"Hi, Stacey," Rosita said flatly. Mark guessed she wasn't a major fan of Stacey's.

"Hey, Rosita, what's up?" Stacey grabbed Laura's arm. "Listen, Laur. You have to come with me. Amanda is upstairs, and we need your advice on something way important."

"I'll find you guys again later," Laura told Rosita. Mark couldn't help but stare at her long legs as she followed Stacey out of the room.

"Okay, what is *up* with you and Laura tonight?" Rosita demanded.

"What are you talking about?" Mark asked, immediately taking his eyes off Laura. "I barely spoke to the girl."

Rosita lifted an eyebrow. "I saw you making eyes at her. I know what you're like when you're on the prowl—"

"The *prowl?*" Mark laughed uncomfortably. "What am I, an animal?"

Rosita didn't flinch. "You can be, sometimes."

Dennis whistled. "Ouch, that hurts."

Man, Rosi could be such a pain. "Look, I don't know what you *thought* you saw," Mark started, leaning back into the sofa. "But Laura isn't my type. So chill, okay?"

25

Rosita's expression softened. "I was just making sure."

"Since I've passed your test, would you mind if I *prowled* a little? I've seen a couple of people that I'd like to . . ." Mark paused, remembering the redhead in the kitchen. "Talk to," he finished.

Rosita rolled her eyes. "Go for it," she told him. She snuggled closer against Dennis. "I think we can entertain each other."

This party was fulfilling every one of Mark's low expectations. He'd successfully avoided Dara for the rest of the evening, but he hadn't been able to find the girl he'd noticed earlier, and his few attempts at flirtation had fizzled—the perky girl with gorgeous eyes had a boyfriend, and the leggy blonde seemed completely uptight. All in all, the freshman class didn't look promising.

I think it's time to get out of here, Mark told himself as he surveyed the almost empty kitchen. *Too bad Doug didn't have another ticket to the game. Even watching baseball would have been better than this party.* He turned to look for Rosita to let her know he was taking off, but right then Dennis tapped him on the shoulder. He looked upset.

"What's wrong?" Mark asked.

Dennis frowned. "Rosi's not feeling too well. We're leaving."

"What's the matter with her?"

"I'm fine," Rosita said weakly, coming up behind Dennis. She looked pale, and she was holding her stomach. "I think I ate too much or something," she explained with an attempt at a smile. "But we have to get Laura. We're her ride home."

"Rosi, we should go *now*," Dennis stated firmly.

"We can't leave without her," Rosita pleaded. "She went upstairs somewhere."

Dennis turned to Mark. "Can you drive Laura home?" he asked.

Drive Laura home. That meant a whole car ride alone with her, trying to make conversation with a girl who came from planet Happy-happy Joy-joy. Still, Rosita looked awful. It was the least he could do.

"Of course," he said.

Rosita and Dennis both looked relieved. "Thanks, Mark," Rosita whispered, her face scrunched up in discomfort. "Tell her I'll call her tomorrow, okay?"

"Yeah, I'll tell her. Just go and feel better." Mark looked at Dennis. "I'll see you later. Take care of her."

Dennis nodded and gently guided Rosita out of the kitchen.

Mark stayed where he was for a moment, debating his next move. He groaned, remembering that he had an early shift at the video store the next day. Maybe he would just find Laura now and get out of this place. He reached over to the table and took a few cookies for the road, then left the room to look for her.

The sooner this night was over, the better.

THREE

"SO ANYWAY, I told her that was ridiculous because who would *want* to go out with Jason Pressman anyway? I mean, really." Amanda widened her eyes to emphasize her utter disbelief.

Laura shook her head to show she understood, even though she really didn't. "That's crazy," she said, squirming in her chair.

When she'd come up here, *hours* ago, she hadn't intended on becoming a prisoner to Amanda's monologues. She'd tried to escape to the bathroom, but it was impossible to get away from these two. Her only hope was that Raphael's older sister would come home and reclaim her room.

Laura glanced at the doorway and was startled to see Mark standing there, looking uncomfortable. His hands were stuffed into the front pockets of his jeans, and he was shuffling from one foot to the other. It was the first time she'd ever seen him appear anything other than cool and cocky. He looked sort of sweet.

Yeah, if you like total flirts, Laura reminded herself.

"Where's Rosita?" she asked, trying to keep her tone casual. She hadn't expected it to be so hard to hang out with Mark. She'd decided long ago that he was bad news, not worth her time. She'd been avoiding him for so long that Rosita had given up on them ever becoming friends.

But tonight, whenever Laura looked at Mark, she became preoccupied with trying to figure out why so many girls went out with him in spite of his reputation. She'd already decided that it could be his dark blue eyes—Laura knew she felt unsettled every time *she* stared into them. There was something so lonely about their expression.

Amanda sat up and smiled when she caught sight of Mark. "The new assistant director!" she exclaimed. "I think it's so cool that Ms. Goldstein is letting you do that. I'm Amanda, by the way. You've probably seen me in rehearsal."

Mark walked into the room, smiling back at Amanda, and—was he checking her out? Laura bit back a frown. "Yeah, I have noticed you," he told her. He was definitely checking her out. Ugh. What was he, the Energizer Bunny of womanizers?

"Stacey, Amanda, there you guys are!" Jill Cherry, the girl most likely to blow out your eardrums with her shrill voice, was standing where

Mark had been a second ago. "You have to come downstairs—there's a drool-worthy guy."

"Um . . ." Amanda still had her eyes on Mark.

"Come *on*," Jill whined.

Laura saw Mark wince at Jill's shrieking. She couldn't help smiling. Clearly Mark shared her opinion of Jill.

"Okay, we're coming," Stacey replied, grabbing Amanda's arm and dragging her off to follow Jill downstairs.

The room suddenly felt very quiet. Laura glanced at Mark. She'd never been alone with him before—it was an unsettling feeling. Where was Rosi anyway?

"Rosita and Dennis had to leave," Mark started, as if guessing her thoughts. "Rosi felt sick, and Dennis wanted to get her out of here. They asked me to drive you home."

"Oh. Okay," Laura said. "Is Rosi all right?"

"I'm sure she'll be fine. She has some kind of stomach thing. She said maybe she ate too much." Mark smirked. "I guess you'll hear about all those chips she pigged out on after all."

Laura smiled. Mark definitely knew Rosi well. "Yeah, I guess so."

He sat down on the bed, staring around at the room. "She said to tell you she'll call you tomorrow." He fiddled with the bedspread.

"Thanks," Laura said, crossing her legs nervously.

There was a long moment of silence. Laura felt more and more uncomfortable by the second. *He's just a guy,* she told herself. *Okay, so you used to like him. And so he's a jerk to girls, but still, you should be able to talk to him like a normal person. Rosita does.*

"Um, so why are you getting involved with the play anyway?" she asked. "I mean, I was just wondering since you've never been in any of them before. And you want to be a writer, like Rosi, right?"

Mark laughed, and Laura couldn't help noting how his blue eyes lit up. Yes, it definitely had to be the eyes that reeled all those girls in.

"You talk really fast," he told her. He paused, holding her gaze.

"Sorry," Laura said.

"It's okay." He gave her a lopsided smile. "I kind of like it."

Laura bit her lip, not sure what to say.

"But yeah, I want to be a writer," Mark went on. "I've always been into writing about people, the way their minds work. And I've always loved movies. So over the summer I started thinking maybe I should go into film—you know, writing and directing. And the play is a good chance to get some directing experience."

He smiled, and Laura saw that he had a dimple in his left cheek. Okay, so maybe it was the eyes *and* the dimple. Were guys like Mark allowed to have dimples? It didn't seem fair. Only nice guys should have dimples.

Mark was watching her with a strange expression on his face.

"Oh," Laura said, suddenly realizing he'd stopped talking. "So how do you like Ms. Goldstein so far?" she asked.

"Do you know that she asked me to rearrange my hours at my job around her rehearsal schedule? She just assumed my boss would *know* that a high-school production is much more important than work."

Laura laughed. "That's nothing," she said. "There was this kid in last year's play whose uncle died, like, a week before opening night. So he had to go to the funeral during one of our last big rehearsals, and Goldstein went psycho on him. She actually told him that he should just go, look at the body, then run back to rehearsal!"

Mark's jaw dropped. "Are you serious?"

Laura nodded. "Totally."

"Well, she can forget pushing me around," he said. "The play's great and all, but bringing home money every week is a lot more important, and she's just going to have to accept that."

The sudden seriousness of Mark's voice caught Laura off guard. Now that she thought about it, she remembered Rosi once telling her that Mark lived alone with his mom and that they seemed to have a hard time making ends meet. "Don't worry," she told him. "Ms. Goldstein is full of insane ideas, but once you set her straight, she deals with it fine. And she's a decent director—her shows always come out well."

Mark nodded. "That's good." He stood up

and walked over to look at a pile of videotapes near the TV.

Laura watched him, wondering if there was more to him than she'd given him credit for before. He obviously didn't have an easy life at home, and he aspired to become a director. . . . Maybe his slimeball reputation wasn't fair. Maybe that was what Rosi was always trying to tell her.

"Oh, look, we've found a Spielberg fan," he announced. "*The Color Purple, E.T., Close Encounters of the Third Kind, Schindler's List.* What else . . ." His voice trailed off as he dug through the movies. "There's some Coppola here too. And a few Oliver Stone pictures."

"You know the directors?" Laura asked, surprised.

Mark put down the tapes and slid down to the floor, leaning his back against the desk. "Of course," he said. "The directors are the ones who craft the films. The director makes or breaks the movie."

"That's not true," Laura argued. "You can have an amazing director and then put some stinky actor in there and the movie's junk. People never say they want to see a *director's* new movie—they always talk about the actors."

"People often say they want to see the new Spielberg movie or whatever," Mark countered. "Besides, you can't measure quality by what people think or say. Most people are ignorant."

"Because they want to see good actors?" Laura asked in disbelief. "Directors *are* important," she continued slowly, "but I don't think you're giving the actors enough credit. Acting is very hard."

Mark was silent for a second. "Is that what you want to do? Am I, like, insulting your life goal here?" Although he said it a little sarcastically, Laura could tell he felt bad.

"No, it's not my life goal," Laura snapped. Mark raised his eyebrows, looking surprised. She went on, softening her tone. "I want to do something more stable than acting, something more reliable."

Mark was watching her with a curious expression on his face—as if he were looking at her for the first time. "I guess the film biz isn't the most secure job choice," he acknowledged. "I kind of worry about that sometimes—about the money. The whole starving-artist thing doesn't thrill me too much."

"Yeah, I know," Laura said. "I've always thought it was silly the way people act like being a poor artist is some romantic life. How are you supposed to do your art when you don't have anywhere to live?"

"Exactly," Mark said, drumming his fingers on the floor. "But starving or not, I wouldn't be happy doing something I didn't love, something I wasn't, I don't know, driven toward. And writing has always been the only way I can—" He stopped, looking down. Then he shook his head a little and glanced back up, smiling.

There were those amazing blue eyes again. *And* the dimple. Laura tried very hard not to stare. "Anyway," he said, "what do you want to do if not acting?"

"I don't know," she admitted, getting out of the

chair and sitting down across from him on the floor. "I'm interested in lots of things. Like foreign affairs. I like learning about other cultures and languages, so my dad said I'd be good at that."

Mark frowned slightly. "Sounds like a cop-out to me."

"Why?" Laura asked. "What's the matter with doing something stable, with having security in your life? You just admitted yourself that it's important."

Mark shrugged. "Foreign affairs doesn't sound like the most creative thing in the world, that's all."

"You don't think learning other languages is creative?" Laura shook her head. "You can tell so much about a culture from the things they have words for. For example, there's a word in Italian for drunk that means 'wine soaked.'"

Mark cocked his head, a thoughtful expression on his face. "Wine soaked? Really?"

Laura nodded, happily surprised that he seemed to find that little tidbit as interesting as she did.

"Huh. I like that," he said. "Okay, so maybe the language part is cool. But wouldn't you miss acting?"

"I guess. But it's not like I could make it as an actor without being gorgeous and knowing all the right people—" Laura stopped, hoping she hadn't somehow offended Mark and his aspirations. "I mean, what you want to do is different. You'd be behind the scenes." Laura cringed. Had she just made it worse? "Not that I'm saying you're not good-looking enough or anything." Okay, was there *any* connection between her brain and her mouth? Because she seriously doubted it right now.

Mark grinned. "You're cute," he said. "You just say everything as soon as it pops into your head, don't you?"

He thinks I'm cute. Laura couldn't help but be excited by his comment. But aloud she said, "You don't?"

"Well . . . no, not really," Mark said, a lock of hair falling across his face. Laura shifted uncomfortably. "I mean, there are things about myself that I don't tell other people. But I get the feeling that you . . . I don't know, that you're different that way."

Laura was suddenly dying to know what those things about himself were. "I guess I am different that way," she finally said. "Are you telling me that I bore people with minor details about myself?"

"Not at all," he said softly. "Exactly the opposite."

Before she could help it, Laura felt her hand reach out to twist the ends of her hair. *No, stop,* she told herself. *He'll know you're nervous.*

"What do you mean?" Laura asked shakily. She had to get ahold of herself. She, Laura Whitman, was definitely not considering liking Mark Adams again!

"It's hard to explain," Mark started, still looking her right in the eye. "But it fascinates me to talk with someone who thinks about things so differently from me."

She *fascinated* him? Had she ever fascinated anyone before? "Wow," she blurted out.

Mark laughed. "See? You're real. I like that."

Maybe people have been exaggerating about what a player he is, Laura thought, gazing back at Mark. *His ex-girlfriends probably just said that stuff about him because they were mad that things didn't work out.*

They were both quiet for a minute, looking at each other.

Maybe he's never met the right girl before, Laura told herself. *Maybe I'm the right girl for him. And he's the right guy for me . . .*

Laura rubbed her shoulder anxiously. *I shouldn't be thinking about him this way,* she reminded herself. *I don't want a guy like Mark.*

"Do you want me to do that?" Mark asked. "My mom taught me a good technique for relaxing muscles."

Laura froze. Did she want him to touch her? More than she would ever admit. But could she actually *let* him? *It's just a little massage,* she rationalized. "Yeah, sure," she responded, trying her hardest to sound nonchalant.

Mark came over and started to massage her neck and shoulders. Laura leaned against him, relaxed and at the same time more alert than she'd ever been in her life. During all the time they'd been here talking, she hadn't even noticed the music. But now as she sat there—barely moving—she heard the old U2 song that was playing downstairs.

"Is this better?" he said softly into her ear.

"Yes," she whispered, afraid to trust herself to speak.

Slowly he turned her toward him, and they faced each other, inches apart.

Laura's breath caught, and the whole room seemed suspended in time. She looked into his eyes, her heart thumping a million beats a minute.

And then he pressed his lips against hers. Laura let herself melt into the kiss, and it was . . . incredible. Explosive. She put her arms around Mark, holding him and shutting out everything but the delicious sensation of his mouth on hers.

Oh my God, oh my God, oh my God, Laura thought over and over a half hour later, her hands clasped tightly in her lap and her gaze fixed on the passenger-side window. They were in Mark's car, on the way back to her house.

"So, uh, I turn at Elm Street, right?" Mark asked her for the third time.

"Yeah, Elm," Laura answered. "You make a left there," she added. What was Mark thinking right now? Why wasn't he talking? Should she say something? "So, um, I hope Rosita's okay," she finally managed to say.

"I'm sure she's fine," Mark said. Laura glanced at his face, hoping he'd turn and smile or give her some kind of reassurance. But instead his eyes stayed glued to the road in front of him, his hands gripping the steering wheel.

"Do you, um, do you want to put on the radio?" Laura tried again. "I mean, I know we like different music, but—"

He shrugged. "Whatever."

Laura blinked, suddenly feeling like she was going to cry. She'd been convinced that something real was developing between them in that room, but maybe she'd just been naive to think that Mark really liked her. Still, when she remembered the way he'd looked at her, the way he'd talked to her so openly, the electricity of their kiss . . .

"I . . . um, I had a good time tonight," she ventured shyly. This was his chance to show he was feeling everything that she was, that things were going to be okay, that she hadn't just been a total idiot and made herself completely vulnerable—

"Could you crack the window open a little?"

That was all he could say? Angry tears stung Laura's eyes. She rolled down the window, silently fuming. How could she have *done* something like this? After the way that girl yelled at him at the party, Laura had still been naive enough to fall for his tricks. She'd actually confused Mark Adams with someone who could be a wonderful boyfriend, just because he'd been a smooth talker. Clearly all the rumors about him were true.

Well, she didn't want someone like Mark anyway— she needed someone dependable, solid, mature.

Someone like Ted Legum.

The realization hit her with so much force that she sucked in her breath. How could she have forgotten all about him, about their date? Somehow that had slipped away from her during those moments in Raphael's sister's bedroom as she looked into Mark's insanely blue eyes.

Mark cleared his throat. "I, uh, I hope you're not thinking what we did tonight was anything too serious," he told her. "I mean, you're really cool and all, but it was just one of those things, right?"

Laura felt another flash of pain and anger rip through her. She'd told herself a year ago that Mark was trouble, and now here he was, proving it. Who did he think he was? And why on earth did she need him when she could have Ted? "Don't worry," she retorted. "I have a date with Ted Legum tomorrow night anyway."

Mark was quiet for a second, and Laura couldn't help but wonder . . . would he ask her not to go? Would he say that he just hadn't known how to act, but that he really did like her?

Then he smiled. "You guys would make a good couple."

Laura blinked back at him, struggling to hide the way each word he uttered felt like another needle sticking into her. How could he be so callous? How could that kiss not have meant anything to him?

"Yeah, I think so too," she replied, fighting back tears. Mark would not see her cry. He would not know that he had gotten to her, that he had made her feel . . . anything. She swallowed, trying to ignore the waves of hurt and humiliation that washed over her.

This night had been the biggest mistake of her life.

FOUR

"LAURA! WAKE UP!" The words slowly seeped into Laura's brain. "Laura!"

She opened her eyes and saw her sister standing in the bedroom doorway, holding the cordless phone in her hand. "Rosita for you," she said, then dropped the phone on the floor before walking away.

Laura got up and ran over to pick up the phone, stumbling over clothes on the floor. "Hello?" she said breathlessly into the receiver. "Rosi? Are you there?"

"Of course I'm here," Rosita answered, laughing. "Sorry I had Julie wake you, but I'm going out soon, and I had to make sure you got home okay last night."

Laura sank onto the floor at the words *last night.* Everything that had happened with Mark came back to her in a horrible rush. Anger, hurt, embarrassment—it all overwhelmed her once again.

"Laur? You're not mad, are you?" Rosita prompted when Laura didn't say anything.

Oh God. How can I tell Rosita? she wondered. It was humiliating. Mortifying.

"Rosi," she started nervously, "there's something I have to tell you." Laura paused, swallowing. "Um, first of all, do you feel better today?" she asked. This was going to be hard.

"Much better," Rosita assured her. "You know how I get those weird stomach things when I eat too much. I felt pretty awful when I got home last night, though."

Laura cringed. There were those words again, *last night*. She let out a little moan.

"What's the matter?" Rosita asked.

There was total silence. "I kissed Mark!" Laura blurted out.

"What?" Rosita exclaimed.

Laura winced and pulled the phone away from her ear. Okay, so she was stupid and naive, but she didn't deserve to go deaf for it.

"I know this is weird for you, Rosi, but it just sort of happened. I thought maybe people were wrong about him, you know?" Why did this sound so much less rational now than it had last night? "I mean, we were talking, and it seemed okay—it seemed right."

"What do you mean . . . right?" Rosita asked.

"I thought that maybe," Laura said weakly, "Mark and I had a real connection."

"You actually thought you and *Mark* could be a

couple?" Rosita asked. The raw disbelief in her voice gave Laura a fresh pang of embarrassment. "But you knew better! You know what he's like!" Rosita paused. "Okay, I'm sorry," she resumed in a quieter tone. "This is just too bizarre. I'm assuming things didn't go very far with Mark, right?"

Laura gasped. "Of course not! Do you think I totally lost my head?"

"Possibly. But anyway, forget about it. And listen to me carefully, Laura—Mark does not want a girlfriend."

"Trust me," Laura said bitterly, "I know. He made that *very* clear to me." Anger began to build up inside her once again. "How do you stand that guy, Rosi? He's such a jerk—he really made me feel . . . He's just a jerk." Laura was too ashamed to admit aloud that Mark had made her feel special. *That's probably how he gets all his girls,* she thought.

"Laur, I'm really sorry. Mark's good as a friend but not as more than that. And trust me, I am not going to let him hear the end of this."

Laura felt new tears collecting in her eyes. "I feel so stupid," she said, her voice cracking. "You warned me, the whole school basically warned me, and I fell for his act anyway." She pulled her knees into her chest, hugging them.

"Please don't cry," Rosita said. "You're going to make me cry. And Mark's not worth it. What about Ted anyway? Aren't you two still on for tonight?"

Laura brightened a little. She and Ted did have a date. A *date.* The word was still powerful enough to cheer her up considerably. "He's picking me up at seven-thirty. But do you think it's still okay to go out with him after what I did?"

Rosita laughed. "Laura, you're adorable. Of course it's okay. Don't even think twice about it. Oh, hold on." She was gone for a second, then came back. "I have to go, sorry. My mom needs me to run some errands. But please, do yourself a favor and forget about this whole Mark mess. Pick out a killer outfit for tonight and have a great time with Ted. And tell me all about it tomorrow." Rosita giggled. "I do want to hear about *Ted's* kisses," she teased.

"Okay. Bye." Laura clicked off the phone and stood up. Determined, she went to her closet and began thumbing through her clothes.

This time, she thought, *I am listening to* everything *Rosita says.*

Yeah, this was fun. The Saturday-morning shift at Video World always left Mark breathless with excitement. Parents with their little kids, yelling and screaming over which movies they could and couldn't see, filled the store's aisles.

Kids his own age didn't start showing up until the evening. Mark forced a smile as a customer approached the register. He mechanically rang up her movie, swiped her membership card, and went through the motions. Oh, well. At least he was getting paid.

The door clanged open behind him, and he turned to see who had walked in. He grinned when he saw Mike and Doug. The two of them always made a funny pair—tall, skinny Doug with his ultrashort, blond hair and tiny features next to Mike's broad build, big eyes, and floppy, dark hair.

"Hey," Mike greeted him. "How's life at the video store?"

Mark rolled his eyes. "The usual." He sighed. "What are you guys up to?"

Doug shrugged. "Are we ever up to anything?" he asked with a lopsided grin. "We were just cruising around and figured we'd check in on you."

"How was the game last night?"

"Oh, man." Mike shook his head. "You wouldn't believe what this idiot here did."

Doug frowned. "Who are you calling an idiot?"

Mark smiled. He loved a good Doug's-an-idiot story.

"He jumped up to catch a fly ball and knocked into the guy next to us. This guy spilled an entire beer right on Doug's head. For the rest of the night he smelled like a brewery," Mike said. "And the guy almost pounded him."

"Yeah, it was the worst," Doug put in. "I was soaked."

"Did you know the word for drunk in Italian means 'wine soaked'?" Mark heard himself ask.

His friends looked at him blankly.

Mark shook his head. Why did *that* pop into his brain?

"So how was the party?" Doug asked.

The party. Laura. Laura's beautiful hazel eyes.

Laura's long, perfect legs. The way she'd looked at him before he kissed her. Kissing her . . .

"It was fine," he answered, trying to keep his voice casual.

"Any action?" Doug asked, wiggling his eyebrows.

"Can't you guys think about anything else?" Mark snapped.

Mike and Doug stared back at him with identical astonished expressions. "It's usually the only thing *you* think about," Mike said.

"Yeah, what are you, Mr. Suddenly Sensitive?" Doug joked. "Since when do you not enjoy telling us all about your latest conquest?"

Mark looked away. What was his problem? What was the big deal? He and Laura had a good time, and now it was over. It wasn't like he'd never done this before.

"Sorry, guys," Mark muttered. "I'm in a weird mood, I guess." He forced a smile. "But no, there was no action."

"Too bad, man," Doug said.

Mark looked down at his feet, wondering why, for the first time ever, he had lied to his best friends about having hooked up with a girl. Why didn't he want to say anything more? *Because she's Rosita's best friend,* he told himself. *That* was why it was none of Mike and Doug's business. After all, it wasn't like he was actually feeling something for Laura Whitman. Her life was totally different from his. Too different.

Besides, she'd made a point of bringing up her

date with Ted Legum. She obviously didn't want anything more from Mark. She probably only kissed him because she'd wanted to break out of her good-girl image for one night. To her, he had been like a little rebellion, a dare. Girls like Laura, who the sun seemed to follow around all the time, never went for guys like him.

And that was just how he wanted it. The last thing Mark needed was for this girl to bug him for the next month, wanting him to take her out and do the whole silly dating thing.

But Mark had to admit, he wouldn't mind hanging out with her—as friends, of course—and learning some more Italian.

"How's your cappuccino?" Ted asked Laura, taking a sip of his mocha latte.

Laura smiled. "Great," she replied. Ted was so thoughtful that he'd asked *her* where she'd like to go for coffee, and it turned out that The Daily Grind was his favorite coffee bar too. Were they a match made in heaven or what? "I really loved the movie," Laura added.

"Me too," Ted said. "I want to be able to act that well someday, don't you?"

See, Ted focuses on the acting, just like I do, Laura thought. Mark had completely written off the actors, as if they weren't the least bit important. What did he know? "There was some pretty amazing acting," she agreed. "Especially that scene with the parents."

"That was my favorite scene too!" Ted exclaimed. He placed his empty mug down in front of him and leaned across the table, closer to Laura. She felt a shiver of excitement. This was what she wanted in a guy—someone who looked out for her every need, who agreed with her—not someone who thought his own opinion ruled. *Not someone like Mark.*

"You know, I had a great time tonight, Laura," Ted told her, his gray eyes soft and gentle.

Laura bit her lip nervously. "So did I."

"I always thought you were a good actress," Ted continued, "but while I was with Emily, I didn't have much time to hang out with the other drama people. Maybe now we'll get to know each other better, especially with us both being leads in the play."

Laura nodded. Ted and Emily had been practically glued at the hip. Laura had always felt a little jealous of relationships like theirs. She'd even envied Rosita's close relationship with Dennis sometimes. Having a boyfriend would make her life absolutely perfect.

Ted glanced at his watch. "I guess we should be getting home," he said reluctantly.

Laura frowned slightly. She never wanted this night to end. A night totally unlike last night. "I guess."

Laura finished her drink quickly, then waited while Ted went to pay the bill. She admired the way he moved across the room, the way he carried himself so confidently. *Could someone like Ted really be interested in me?* Laura wondered in awe.

As Ted drove her home, Laura couldn't help but compare this ride with the one in Mark's car the night before. With Mark she had felt nervous and scared. But she felt safe here with Ted—he wasn't going to turn all weird or act like she didn't mean anything to him. He was even steering with one hand to keep the other one free to hold hers.

When Ted pulled up in front of Laura's house ten minutes later, she hated the thought of having to say good-bye and walk inside.

"I guess I'll see you at rehearsal on Monday," he said quietly, his eyes fixed on hers.

Laura smiled. "Yeah." Then before she knew it, he'd scooted over the seat and was reaching to pull her closer to him. Laura closed her eyes and waited for his kiss.

When his lips met hers, she felt a flash of confusion. She'd expected electricity, excitement—the things she'd felt kissing Mark. But this just felt sort of strange and awkward. Angry at herself for comparing them, Laura kissed Ted back more forcefully. *This* was what a good kiss was supposed to be like, she told herself. Mark had just gotten things all jumbled up in her head, and it was going to stop. Now.

Ted finally pulled back, a silly grin on his face. "Wow," he said. "You're a great kisser."

At least it was dark, so he couldn't see the red blotches that she knew had appeared on her cheeks. "Thanks," she answered shyly.

"So, I'll see you Monday?"

"Yeah, Monday." Laura gave him one last smile, then started to open the car door.

"Laura?" She turned back, swallowing hard. "I really did have fun tonight," Ted told her.

"Me too," she said, then hurried out of the car and into her house before she did something really goofy, like skip across the front lawn out of happiness.

Laura floated up the stairs and into her bedroom, flopping down onto the bed. Bliss. That's what this was—total, unending bliss. Her life was perfect.

Well, almost. Laura frowned, remembering that she'd have to face Mark on Monday at rehearsal. He'd probably be cold to her—rude and aloof like he'd been in the car. Or worse, he'd grin at her with a look of satisfaction because he'd *had* her. The thought made her sick.

No, Laura told herself sternly. *I will not let Mark ruin another night of my weekend. Tonight was more than I ever dreamed it could be, and Ted is the only person who matters.*

And with that she changed into shorts and a T-shirt, climbed under the sheets, and drifted off to sleep, forcing herself not to think about anything except for how unbelievably happy she was with Ted.

LAURA AND MARK MEET, POSTKISS
A play in one act, written and directed by
Laura's Subconscious Mind

Take One:
[Laura walks into rehearsal, sees Mark and

Ted together, talking. Laura looks on in horror.]

MARK:
Oh, hey, Laura. I was just filling Ted in on how easy you are. *[Leering smile]*
[Laura runs out, screaming]

Take Two:
LAURA:
Hi, Mark.
[Mark is silent]

LAURA:
[screaming in Mark's ear] Mark! Mark! Hello?

[Mark looks straight through her as if she isn't there]

MS. GOLDSTEIN:
Come on, Laura, you *know* that Mark doesn't talk to girls after he's hooked up with them. In fact, maybe it would be a good idea if you quit the play. Amanda, would you like to take over the lead?
[Laura runs out, screaming]

Take Three:
MARK:
You know, Laura, I really felt something for you the other night. I never wanted a girlfriend before, but now I do.

LAURA:

[happily] You mean it? So I wasn't just being a naive fool?

MARK:

[bursts into laughter, joined by the rest of the cast, suddenly standing around them] Ha! Of course I don't mean it. I was totally using you, and you actually fell for it! Isn't she stupid, everyone? [Loud agreement from cast]

[Laura runs out, screaming]

FIVE

"I CANNOT BELIEVE you hit on my best friend," Rosita announced the minute Mark walked into their creative-writing class on Monday morning.

Mark groaned. He should have expected this, but ever since the party he'd been trying not to think about his kiss with Laura. Thinking about Laura meant wondering how her date with Ted had gone. And the idea of Laura kissing that guy—kissing *any* guy—was strangely upsetting.

"How could you do that to Laura?" Rosita asked as he slid into the chair next to hers. "She's my best friend."

"I know, Rosi, I'm sorry," he said. Usually Rosita was cool with his being such a flirt, but this time he could tell she was really upset. "It just . . . happened."

Rosita sighed. "Look, Mark, Laura isn't like the

55

other girls you go out with. She wants something real, an actual relationship. And you only want to play around."

Mark gave her his best apologetic puppy-dog look. "I said I was sorry," he told her. "But it's not like I set out to fool around with Laura. I would never intentionally hurt your friend."

"Then why did you do it?" Rosita asked.

Mark shrugged uncomfortably, remembering Laura's face so close to his, her lips so soft and kissable. "I don't know. She just got to me or something."

Rosita regarded him silently.

"You said yourself she's not like other girls!" Mark burst out, unable to stand Rosita's scrutiny. "Usually I hang out with airheads—I admit it. And Laura's not like that. She took me by surprise, and I messed up. What do you want me to say?"

Finally Rosita smiled. "I want you to say you'll get over your big fear of commitment and get yourself a real girlfriend."

"Not a chance." Mark winked at her. "I'm having too much fun."

Rosita pulled out her notebook and opened it, signaling the end of this conversation. "You just better be nice to Laura and not make her feel any worse than she does," she said.

"I'll be nice," he promised. "I'll be her best friend ever. Wait and see."

Breathe in, breathe out. Breathe in, breathe out, Laura told herself as she prepared to go into rehearsal Monday after school. This technique was supposed to work for calming frantic people down, right? *Breathe*—wait, was it in or out this time?

"This is not a big deal," Laura muttered, heading down the hallway toward the theater. "I am a mature person, and I can handle this." Sure, that was why she'd dreamed that Ms. Goldstein had kicked her out of the play for kissing Mark. Laura stood still a moment, smoothing down her short-sleeved cardigan to keep her hands from reaching for the ends of her hair. *Why didn't I wear a ponytail today?* she wondered in agony. Then she took one final deep breath, pushed open the backstage door, and walked into the theater.

Mark was the only person in the auditorium.

This can't be happening, she thought in horror. Someone really hated her—or at least wanted to watch her suffer intensely.

Laura paused at the top of the stairs, debating whether or not to turn around and leave. *No, that would be silly,* she scolded herself. As if standing there frozen in place was a real improvement.

Mark turned around. She braced herself for the expression he'd have on his face, for the self-satisfied smirk. But instead she saw a . . . smile? Mark was *smiling* at her in a completely innocent way?

"Hey, Laura," Mark called. "What's up?" There wasn't a trace of annoyance or dread in his voice, just sheer friendliness.

"Hi," Laura managed to say. Still unsure, she

walked down the stage steps slowly, then sat down a few seats away from him.

"How was your weekend?" he asked. "What did you and Ted end up doing?"

She paused. "We went to see *Way of the Road*." Laura crossed her legs and eased back into the seat, willing herself to not move her fingers anywhere near the vicinity of her hair.

"Really?" Mark asked, raising his eyebrows. "I want to see that. How was the *acting?*" He put extra emphasis on the last word, and Laura laughed in spite of herself.

"It was really good." She hesitated, confused. Why was he being nice? And why was *she?* Wasn't she furious with him? "I kind of paid extra attention to the directing too," she admitted. "You were right—I could see how directing has an effect on the way scenes come across." Laura's words surprised even herself a bit. She hadn't realized that she'd given any thought to this during the movie.

Mark looked impressed. "I converted you that easily?" he asked, his smile widening.

"No," she retorted. "I still think you're wrong about actors. This movie would've been completely different without Kevin Spacey in the lead." She watched him, waiting for a sneer, a smirk—anything so that she could stay mad. But he simply looked back at her with that same open expression. "I'm just saying that you showed me that other parts of the movie are also worth looking at," she finished.

Mark sighed. "I never said actors don't matter. I think they do, a lot. After all," he continued, his eyes twinkling, "*Only Today* would be a very different play without you and Ted, right?"

Laura giggled, feeling herself loosen up. "Without me, this play would be nothing," she announced dramatically.

"Less than nothing," Mark joked.

Okay, she thought. *I can do this. I can joke around with him. Just forget that anything ever happened.* "So, how was *your* weekend?" she asked, settling deeper into her seat.

Mark shrugged. "I had to work at the video store, always a joy. And yesterday I tried to work on my screenplay scene for creative writing. I can't seem to come up with any good ideas, though. It's really frustrating."

Laura nodded. "Rosita tells me about writer's block. It sounds tough."

"It is." Mark ran a hand through his dark hair. "You write sometimes, don't you?"

"Not really . . . why?"

"I guess I assume that people who really think about things—the way you seem to—would write."

Laura gave him a half smile. "I don't exactly have a way with words."

Mark shook his head. "What are you talking about? That wine-soaked thing you told me about was so cool. I kept thinking about it over the weekend—it made me want to learn Italian."

Laura regarded Mark, wondering what was

59

going on inside his head. He'd really thought that much about something she said? But hadn't it all been an act that night? She'd assumed that he pretended to enjoy talking to her just so that he could score with her. But now he was acting like he really wanted to be friends.

"Hey, look who just walked in," Mark said.

Laura turned to see Ted coming down the steps. She jumped, startled. If Ted saw her sitting with Mark, what would he think? Would he be able to tell somehow that she'd kissed him?

"Maybe you should go sit by your muffin-toast," Mark teased.

Her *what?* Laura felt her cheeks flush. "Maybe I will." She stood up uncertainly, catching Ted's eye. Ted smiled broadly and motioned for her to come over.

A wave of relief washed over her. Of course Ted didn't know anything about her and Mark. And seeing a guy like Ted beckon to her was enough to put a genuine smile on her face.

"I'll see you around," Mark said behind her.

"See ya," Laura murmured, then walked over to Ted.

"What were you doing with Adams?" Ted asked her as soon as she sat down. "I thought you hated him."

Oh, boy. Laura played with her hands in her lap. "Well, um, I have to be nice to him because of Rosita."

"Oh. Bummer." Ted seemed satisfied. "How's your day been?"

"Good, it's been good." She gulped, trying to calm herself down. Being in the same room with two guys she'd kissed within the space of twenty-four hours was a situation she'd never imagined she'd find herself in. It certainly wasn't a welcome one. "What about yours?"

"Kind of annoying, actually," Ted began. He went on to describe problems he was having with his physics class, and Laura listened with what she hoped was an attentive expression on her face. But she had trouble focusing on his words. She kept replaying her conversation with Mark, trying to understand why talking to him had been so easy. And so normal. Wasn't she supposed to hate him?

"So, I think I'm just going to have to switch sections," Ted finished.

Laura nodded. "Good idea," she said.

And she was sure it was, even though she had no clue why or what he had just told her.

Laura practically fell into the sofa the second she walked into her house that evening. She closed her eyes, replaying her day in her mind.

If someone had asked her on Saturday, she would have sworn she never wanted to see Mark again. But after their short interaction today she had to admit that she kind of liked the idea of getting to know him better. So far, she was interested in pretty much everything he'd ever said to her. Okay, so maybe he was an immature jerk when it came to girls, but that didn't mean they couldn't be friends, right? After all, Rosi was friends with him. . . .

"Hey, lazy." Laura opened her eyes and sat up. Her sister was standing before her.

Laura smiled. "Hi, Jules, how are you?" Julie's wavy, brown hair was unbrushed and messy. She looked exhausted.

"I'm fine," Julie answered, a defensive edge to her voice. "Why?"

Laura frowned. "Since when does there have to be a reason for me to ask what's going on with you?"

Julie sat down on the other end of the couch and began playing with the throw pillow. "It just seemed like you were grilling me or something," she mumbled.

Grilling her? With one innocent question? Something was definitely up with her sister. "Julie," Laura started gently, "did something happen? You know you can tell me anything." She edged closer to her sister.

Julie laughed, but it sounded forced. "No, nothing happened," she said. "I told you—I'm fine." She brushed a strand of hair out of her face and smiled at Laura. "At least I would be if you would stop acting like I'm a space alien with a deadly virus or something."

Laura couldn't help but smile back. "Sorry. I just want to make sure everything's okay."

Julie groaned. "Everything's great, Laur. What wouldn't be? Why don't you fill me in on all of *your* news?"

Laura paused. Should she tell her little sister about Mark? She hadn't said anything to Julie about him so far. But of course she had already told her all about Ted. "Okay," she said. "So, I didn't know what things would be like with Ted today, you know?"

Julie nodded.

"Well, it was incredible! I mean, he walked into rehearsal and immediately asked me to come sit by him. Then he put his arm around me." As Laura said all this aloud, the elation she'd felt earlier today washed back over her again.

Julie smiled. "That's great."

The phone rang, and Julie sighed. "I'm sure it's for you," she teased, getting up to answer it anyway. "It's Rosita!" she yelled from the kitchen a second later.

Laura jumped up and ran into the kitchen. "Thanks," she told Julie, taking the receiver from her. "We'll hang out later, okay?"

"Yeah, sure," she called over her shoulder as she left.

Laura watched her go, then focused on the phone in her hand. "Hey, Rosi."

"I have the worst news, Laur," Rosita wailed.

"What's wrong?"

"Dennis's family has a trip planned for the weekend of my birthday!"

Laura let out a sigh, relieved that nothing catastrophic had occurred. "God, Rosi, you had me thinking someone had died or something."

"But you know how I am about birthdays."

This was true—Rosita treated them like worldwide holidays. "You're right. I'm sorry," Laura said.

"I don't know what to do," Rosita moaned. "I mean, no offense, but you and I just sitting around hanging out somewhere isn't really what I'd been hoping for."

"Well, maybe you can have a party before he goes," Laura suggested.

Rosita let out a heavy sigh. "This is the last time I have a weekend birthday for another, like, seven years. I want to do something on my actual birthday."

Laura couldn't help feeling a little frustrated. When Rosi got like this, there was nothing anyone could say to comfort her. "Um, listen, Rosi, I can't really talk now," she said. "I was kind of in the middle of something with Julie. But I'm sorry about the birthday thing. We'll think of something—don't worry. Talk to you later?"

"Okay." Rosita sounded unconvinced.

Laura hung up the phone and stared out the window. What could she do to make Rosita's birthday special? *Something to totally take her mind off Dennis,* she thought. *If that's possible.* Dinner at some great restaurant? No, that would only remind her that she should be out on a date with Dennis. A girls-only slumber party? No, it would just turn into an all-night talk session about boys—and *that* would remind her of Dennis.

But not if it was a big party with girls and guys, Laura realized. *If Rosi got busy dancing and socializing, she wouldn't have time to miss Dennis. That's it!*

Laura chewed on her lip, thinking. Planning parties wasn't her specialty. But there was no reason she had to do it alone—she'd just call someone else to help her! Someone else who was friends with

Rosita too, like maybe . . . "Sara," she said out loud. "I'll call Sara."

But Sara wasn't home, and neither was Berna. Erica's line was busy (hadn't they heard of call waiting?), and Jeanna's mom was on their other line.

Who else was left? Dennis wouldn't be any help since he was going away.

There's always Mark, she reminded herself. She *could* call Mark. It wouldn't be like a social call or anything. Mark was one of Rosita's close friends, after all. He'd be a big help in knowing what kind of party she'd like. And besides, he could invite their other friends from the literary magazine— Laura didn't know those people too well or which ones Rosi would want to invite. But Mark would know.

Really, it all made perfect sense. It was extremely logical. She would call Mark. It wasn't like she *wanted* to call him or anything. She really didn't have any other choice.

Pink Floyd's *The Wall* was turned all the way up, but its usual inspirational effect wasn't working for Mark tonight. He looked at the blank screen of his word processor, wondering when he'd ever have an idea. Correction—an idea that hadn't already been done. Mark sighed, dropping his head down on the desk.

The phone rang, jolting him out of his thoughts. "Hello?" he answered.

The person at the other end was silent.

"Hello?" he repeated, getting irritated. Was Doug pranking him again?

"Uh, hi, is this Mark?" Nope, not Doug. But very possibly a girl he didn't want to talk to right now.

"Who's this?" he asked.

"Laura."

Laura? Why on earth was *she* calling him? "Oh, hi. Yeah, it's Mark."

"Hi. I was, well, I was actually calling about Rosita. I mean, her birthday is coming up, you know, and she just called me a little while ago to tell me that Dennis is going to be away for it, so she's pretty upset."

This girl talked *so* fast. Mark smiled to himself. He had to admit, Laura was pretty cute, the way she had so much energy.

"So I had this idea that we could throw her a surprise party the Saturday after next. Don't you think she would like that?" Laura finally stopped for air.

Oh, boy, Mark thought. *She is such the upbeat do-gooder.* He shook his head, still smiling. But Laura was right—Rosita was a total party hound, and this would definitely make her birthday. "That's nice of you," he said. "Good idea."

"Would you mind helping me out with stuff?" Laura asked nervously. She sounded like she expected him to try to eat her arm or something.

"Sure, no problem," he replied in what he

hoped was his least scary voice. "What do you want to do?"

"I was thinking maybe you could come over tomorrow after school and we could figure out how to do this—get together a guest list and everything. I mean, if you're not busy or something. I'd completely understand if you can't come. Really."

Laura paused, obviously waiting for his response. Go to this girl's house? Enter the land of the abnormally normal? Well, it would be an experience.

Of course, tomorrow afternoon he was supposed to be "studying" with a cute freshman he'd met during lunch today. But somehow hanging out with Laura seemed more interesting. And after all, it was for Rosita.

"No, I'm not busy," Mark answered. "Tomorrow afternoon would be fine."

"Okay, great. So, I'll see you tomorrow?"

"Yeah, see you then. Bye." Mark hung up the phone, turning back to his blank screen. He started typing absentmindedly, then stopped and looked at what he'd written: *Laura Whitman has a very sexy voice.*

He immediately held down the delete key until the screen was empty again.

SIX

LAURA CHECKED HERSELF in the mirror above her cherry-oak dresser, smoothing down her long, brown hair. Why was she trying so hard to look nice anyway? *I would be doing this for anyone,* she told herself. *It's just polite to look your best when you have company.* That's what her mother always said. Was it her, or did her lips look a little too pale? She didn't want the guy to think she was sick or anything. Laura reached for her spice lipstick, the one Rosita had told her brought out the green in her eyes, and quickly applied it.

The sound of the doorbell made her jump. She spritzed herself with some perfume, then ran downstairs to let Mark in.

When she opened the door, Mark was standing on her porch, looking as nervous as he had the night of the party. He was wearing faded blue jeans with a gray T-shirt that made his eyes look a lighter shade of blue than usual. Not that she was keeping track of the different *hues* of his eye color or anything . . .

"Hi . . . come on in," Laura said, stepping back from the door.

Mark walked inside hesitatingly, as if he thought there might be a bouncer waiting to kick him back out. "Your house is very nice," he told her, looking around the living room.

"Thank you," Laura replied awkwardly, wondering if this had been a completely terrible idea. "Come on up to—" She stopped herself midsentence. Usually whenever Rosita or another friend came over, they would just hang out in her bedroom. But she certainly couldn't invite Mark there. "To the den," she finished. "We can talk there."

Mark followed her upstairs and into the family den.

"Sit down," she told him, waving loosely at the black leather couch. He did so, gingerly. Laura plopped down across from him in the matching recliner.

Mark sniffed the air. "Something smells good," he said. "Like flowers."

"Um . . . we just cleaned the house," Laura blurted out. "That must be what you're smelling— lavender-scented cleaning stuff." If he thought she'd put on perfume, he'd assume it was for him— and it definitely wasn't. She simply enjoyed smelling like flowers.

Mark shrugged. "Where's the rest of your family?" He glanced around the room, and Laura watched him take in all of her parents' diplomas. Her mom and dad both had Ph.D.'s. They needed one whole wall to fit their degrees and certificates.

"My parents are at work," Laura explained, "and my sister Julie's taking a nap." Coming home and going straight to sleep until dinner was a new habit of Julie's. Laura figured maybe she'd been acting weird lately because she was just overtired or something. "So, about the party. I was thinking you and I could both write down names of people Rosita would want there and then combine them to make sure we've got everybody."

"Sounds good," Mark agreed. "Where are we going to have it?"

"Huh, I hadn't even thought of that," Laura said, feeling like a supreme idiot. A party without a location wouldn't exactly be a huge success.

"Well, what about here?" Mark asked. "You certainly have the space for it," he added with a snort.

"Why do you make that sound like a bad thing?" Laura asked, surprised.

Mark turned away from her, focusing on the floor. "It's not. This house was made for throwing parties. I guess I just . . ." He raised his eyes back up to hers, then continued. "I kind of feel overwhelmed in places like this, that's all."

Overwhelmed in her home? That seemed pretty

bizarre. "Why? What's your house like?" she asked.

Mark scowled. "Are you worried I come from the projects or something?"

Laura felt like she'd been slapped. "No, that's not what I was . . . never mind." She glanced down at the floor, tracing the pattern on the carpet with her foot.

"I'm sorry." Mark sighed. "I didn't mean to be so harsh. I live over near Bloomfield, in an apartment with my mom."

Laura looked at him again. He had a sincerely apologetic expression on his face. "Fine," she told him. "Let's just get back to Rosi's party, all right?"

Mark smiled, looking more relaxed. "Yeah, sure."

There was that dimple again. Laura tried not to focus on it. "Well, we definitely need decorations."

Mark laughed, running a hand through his dark hair. "Decorations. Of course."

Laura could feel her cheeks flush at Mark's teasing response. "Hey—are you making fun of me?"

Mark continued to smile, his blue eyes lighting up just as they had the other night. "No, not at all. Decorations are a must for any party."

"You *are* making fun of me!" Laura protested. Still, she was grinning despite herself. "I'll have you know that decorating's very important to Rosita. If we don't buy decorations, we might as well—"

"I know, I know." Mark laughed, cutting her off. "You don't need to convince me."

"Oh." Laura was taken aback. "I don't?"

Mark shook his head, smile *and* dimple still intact. "Do you want to go shopping for them Friday afternoon?"

Laura blinked back at him. Was he actually offering to go with her to pick out the decorations? *I guess we really are going to be friends,* Laura thought. "Sure. That's good with me."

"Cool," Mark said. He glanced around the den again. "So, what time do your parents get home anyway?"

Laura watched Mark as he zeroed in on a family photo on the shelf next to him. "My mom gets home at five-thirty, and my dad gets back around six," she told him.

"That must be nice," he said, looking back to Laura. "My mom doesn't come home until much later. She works insane hours."

"Oh. That must be hard for you," Laura said cautiously, afraid that he might blow up at her again.

"Yeah, it kind of is," he admitted. "She has a lot of health problems, so I worry about her working so much." He paused, letting out a sigh. "It's pretty tough, watching her destroy herself to support us and not being able to tell her to stop, because we need the money."

Laura couldn't even imagine being in his shoes. "Wow," she whispered. "My parents both work hard, but they love their jobs. My mom's a professor, and my dad works at an engineering company."

"Yeah, well, you're really lucky," Mark said grimly. "Most people *don't* live like this." He gestured around at the room.

Laura felt a surge of resentment. He always seemed to be judging her, as if he thought she was some kind of spoiled princess. "Okay, so I'm lucky," she said. "Does that mean I should feel guilty or something? Because you seem to think so." Mark didn't respond—he just stared back at her blankly.

"You know what else?" she continued. "I'm not the only person in the world whose parents are still married and like their jobs and make enough money. Plenty of people have happy families. Just because you—" She cut herself off, wishing she could take back those last words. Why did she have such a big mouth?

Mark didn't even flinch. "Just because what?" he challenged. "Just because I don't have a father? Well, the jerk left us before I could crawl and doesn't seem to think child support applies to him. So maybe I do have reason to believe that things don't go perfectly for everyone—that life can stink."

Laura gulped. God, what would that be like, to never have known her dad? The thought was scary, even terrifying. "I'm so sorry," Laura said. "I didn't mean to—I didn't mean to say that." She stared at Mark, feeling an urge to make everything better for him. "I can understand where you're coming from," she started slowly. "If I'd been through what you have, I would've—well, I don't even know what I would've done. But you can't hate *everyone* for what your father did to you and your mom."

Mark studied his hands. "That's easier said than done."

Laura moved to the sofa, sitting down next to him. "Have you ever seen your dad since he left?" she asked softly.

"No," Mark replied in a tight voice. "He sent me a couple of birthday cards and stuff when I was younger. He always said he loved me and that I should try to understand why he couldn't be with me." Mark shook his head, pushing his long hair away from his face. "How on earth is a five-year-old supposed to grasp something like that?"

Laura bit her lip, gaining a whole new understanding of Mark. No wonder he couldn't stay with a girl for more than a day. After the way his dad had treated him, he probably didn't trust anyone in the world.

"I called him once," Mark continued. "I got his phone number from a cousin of his who stays in touch with my mom."

"What happened?" Laura asked.

"Some woman answered. We talked for a long time, and she said my dad always went on about his son, that he was so proud of me. God, it was pathetic how happy I was." Mark laughed bitterly.

Laura reached out to grab his hand. "That is *not* pathetic," she argued, squeezing his fingers. Mark's eyes widened. He was clearly surprised by her action, but he didn't pull his hand back. "What happened then?" she asked.

"This is the ultimate in pitiful," Mark began, looking away from her and out the window. "She said she was sure he'd want to call me back right away. So I waited, and I kept thinking, 'Dad hasn't called back yet, but I *know* he will because that lady said he would be so excited to hear from me.'" His voice sounded strained, as if he was on the verge of tears. Then he turned back to Laura. "Surprise, surprise," he said. "Dad never called back." Laura was silent—she didn't know what to say. How could a man never want to speak to his own son?

Mark shook his head, as if he were shaking away the bad memory. "Anyway. At least I learned not to get my hopes up about stuff like that ever again," he said, his voice suddenly sounding much lighter. "I mean, think of it this way: If I expect the worst, the only way I'll ever be surprised is happily." He gave Laura a crooked smile.

Laura could hear the pain behind Mark's forced bright tone. And she could still see the sadness in his eyes, even though he was smiling. "You're wrong," she told him gently. "You're so sure of your doom that you wouldn't even see something good in your life if it was right in front of you. You're blind to anything that could make you happy."

Mark lifted his eyebrows, looking startled, and

Laura wondered if her words had actually gotten through to him. He stared at her for a long moment—hard, without saying a word.

Then he glanced away, clearing his throat. "Why don't we get started on the guest list?" he asked. Laura's hand was still on top of Mark's, and he moved it now, reaching for the notebook on the coffee table in front of him.

Laura blinked back at him, taken off guard by his abrupt change of subject. Hanging out with Mark was definitely a surprise from one moment to the next—you never knew how he was going to act.

"Well . . . there's Sirin Thada," Laura began. She watched Mark as he wrote down the name. What was going on inside his head? He glanced up at Laura, obviously waiting for her to say another name. "Um, who else? Maybe Abby Cohen?" she suggested.

Mark shifted in his seat, looking uncomfortable. "Uh, okay," he said.

Suddenly an image of Mark and Abby popped into her head. An image of them standing near her homeroom, kissing.

Oh God, right. How could Laura have forgotten that Abby had preceded her as one of the notches in Mark's belt! She winced. It didn't make any sense the way Mark could be two different people. He was this sensitive, emotional guy, but he was also a player who fooled around with any girl stupid enough to fall for his act.

"Laura? Your phone's ringing."

"Huh?" Startled out of her thoughts, she suddenly heard the ringing of the phone. "Oh, right," she said, reaching over to pick it up. "Hello?" she said, trying her hardest to sound normal. Mark was not going to know he had upset her.

"Hi, Laura?"

It was Ted! Laura couldn't help the smile from spreading across her face. It was just so cool to hear his voice on the phone. "Hey, Ted."

"Hey. I got your number from the drama-club phone list. Are you busy?"

"Actually, I am sort of in the middle of something," Laura replied. "But I should be done soon. Can I call you back?"

"Sure. I was really just calling to ask if you wanted to hang out Saturday night anyway. How does that sound?"

Laura's heart jumped. A second weekend in a row—did this mean they were a real couple now? "Saturday night would be great," Laura answered, probably a little more loudly than she needed to. It couldn't hurt to let Mark know that she was in demand. "I'll call you later, and we can talk more, okay?"

"Okay, great. Bye, Laura."

"Bye." Laura hung up the phone and turned back to face Mark. "That was Ted," she explained stupidly.

Mark smiled. "That's cool."

Laura smiled back at him. "Yeah, it is," she said.

The room suddenly grew quiet. For what seemed like the millionth time, Mark glanced around the den. Laura reached up and grabbed the ends of her hair.

A door slammed downstairs. Laura looked over at the grandfather clock against the wall. 5:32. Her mom was home.

"I guess I should be going," Mark said quickly, standing up.

"Okay, sure. I'll walk you downstairs. You can meet my mom." She stood up too, taking the notebook from him. "I'll hold on to this," she said. "Are we still on for the mall on Friday?"

Mark nodded. "Yeah."

They clomped downstairs together in silence. Somehow Laura wasn't surprised when Mark bolted out of the house as soon as she introduced him to her mom. He barely stopped to say hello. As soon as he was gone, her mom looked at her questioningly.

"So how do you know Mark?" she asked.

How could she explain to her mom who he was? The guy she kissed at a party without even knowing him at all? A friend? "He's a friend of Rosita's," she finally said. "We're planning a surprise party for her."

Her mom smiled. "Oh, that's nice. Where are you having it?"

"Um, here?" Laura asked, doing her best impression of an angelic-daughter look.

Mrs. Whitman laughed. "Here is fine," she

answered. "Just let me know the date and what's involved."

"Thanks, Mom!" Laura threw her arms around her mother, hugging her tightly. After everything Mark had said about his parents, she felt extra grateful for what she had.

And I might not know how to explain Mark to Mom, Laura thought, pulling away from her mother and smiling, *but I definitely know what to say about Ted!*

SEVEN

"HOW CAN YOU say that?" Laura cried in anguish. "Peter, don't you know how much you mean to me?"

Ted sighed. "You know I can't trust you, Samantha," he said in a flat voice. "Not after what happened at the dance."

Laura bit her lip, trying to hide her frustration. She and Ted were supposed to be practicing their lines while Ms. Goldstein rehearsed two other actors, but Ted just didn't seem into it. He delivered every line straight from the script, but his words didn't convey the emotions his character, Peter, was feeling.

"Um, maybe we should take a break," Laura suggested.

"Good idea." Ted sank onto the couch in the backstage dressing room, where they had gone to rehearse. "It feels like we're practically in every scene, doesn't it?"

"Yeah, it does," she agreed, sitting down next to him. Ted was right; they were in a ton of scenes. But Laura loved it—it was the first time she'd ever had that "problem." *I guess being a lead is just old news for Ted,* she thought.

"Have you gotten out of your physics section yet?" Laura asked him. She loved that she knew what was going on in Ted's life and in his head. It made her feel in control, as if nothing could catch her off guard with him. *Unlike with other people,* she told herself, thinking back to the ups and downs of her conversation with Mark the other day.

Ted frowned. "No, not yet." He stretched his left arm out and let it hang behind Laura's back. She couldn't get over how exciting it was to have Ted do little things like that, things that showed her and everyone else that they were together. He still hadn't said anything to make it official, but every day at rehearsal they sat next to each other and he would hold her hand or put his arm around her. And he'd called her every night that week.

"So, what are you going to do? Are you going to try and switch?" Laura leaned into Ted, resting her head on the side of his shoulder. He tightened his arm around her, and she felt secure, safe.

"I don't know. Maybe I'll just stick it out. Things are getting a little better." He reached his right arm around and lifted her face with his hand, tilting her head toward his. "You know, no one else is around right now," he whispered.

Chills went down Laura's spine, and she felt herself blush. "What do you mean?"

Ted leaned down and brushed her lips with a brief kiss. He tasted like . . . perfection. Her frustration with him melted away as she got lost in the romance of their little private moment together.

"This is the part of rehearsal I look forward to," Ted murmured. "Being close to you."

There it went again—her ever increasing heart rate. Laura took a deep breath, getting used to resorting to the technique for slowing down her pulse.

"Ted, Laura, back onstage. We're going to run scene four," Ms. Goldstein's voice bellowed out.

Laura scrambled out of her seat, her cheeks burning. She really hoped her drama teacher didn't know what they were doing back here. Laura suddenly wondered if Ted used to do this with Emily during rehearsals.

Pushing the thought away, she hurried out onto the stage.

"Mark, why don't you try blocking this scene?" Ms. Goldstein suggested.

Laura stopped in her tracks, a strange churning sensation in her stomach. Mark turned to look at her from where he was sitting in the wings. He caught her eye and gave her an encouraging smile. She tried to smile back but suddenly felt very anxious.

Ted walked to center stage, but Laura couldn't

move. It was as if she were glued in place.

"Come on, Laura," Ted urged, coming back over to her. "What's wrong?" He followed her eyes to Mark, then looked back at her with a puzzled expression. "Do you still have a problem with him?"

Laura shook her head. "Of course not," she said quickly. "Why would I?"

Ted didn't look convinced. "Are you sure you're okay?" he asked, squinting.

"I'm fine," Laura promised. She took his hand and followed him upstage, trying to ignore the burning in her back where she could feel Mark's eyes on her.

Mark listened as Laura delivered her lines, amazed at the power the words took on when she recited them. It felt like it wasn't even Laura up there, but Samantha Roberts, her character. Ted's performance, on the other hand, didn't ring true. Mark could see how people would think Ted was an okay actor because he never missed a cue. But it didn't seem like he was *feeling* it all, deep down. *That's probably because Legum doesn't have a "deep down."*

"Try moving closer to her," Mark instructed as he watched Ted's movements. "What she's saying is really affecting you, so let it show in your body." Mark glanced at Ms. Goldstein for approval, and she nodded to show she agreed. He loved watching the play take on life and knowing he was shaping it.

But as the scene continued, Mark realized he was having trouble keeping his focus. Laura had such an incredible stage presence—something about her was just very . . . watchable. *Those short shorts of hers aren't helping,* he thought miserably. Why was he still so attracted to her?

Focus, Adams, focus, Mark told himself, shaking his hair out of his face. *You're the director.* "Okay, Laura, I need to see the tension more in your upper body at this point," he said, trying to keep his voice even.

She wrinkled her forehead, looking confused. "What do you mean?" she asked.

"Go show her," Ms. Goldstein told him. "Sometimes you have to get up there onstage and position the actors' bodies yourself."

"Um, okay," Mark said, as if it was no big deal. Which it wasn't, really.

He hopped onto the stage and walked over to Ted and Laura, stopping in front of her. He noticed Ted frowning at him.

"Just grab her arms!" Ms. Goldstein yelled in her usual subtle way.

Laura gave him a half smile, holding out her arms. Were they shaking? It was probably just the stage lights. Mark swallowed, then reached out to touch her, putting his hands right below the ends of her T-shirt sleeves. A charge went through his body as his fingers closed around her skin. Couldn't it have been winter, so she wouldn't have had so much skin exposed?

"I just meant . . . sort of like this," Mark said, moving Laura's arms the way he pictured they should be for the scene. When he had them in the position he wanted, he looked her right in the eye, his face inches away from hers. "Do you see what I'm saying?" he asked, his voice barely above a whisper. Her mouth was so close to his that he could feel her breath on his neck.

"Yeah, I think I get it," Laura answered. She was looking at him intensely, and it was all he could do not to move his hands around her back and pull her against him.

"You can let go now, Mark." Ted's hard-edged words cut into Mark's thoughts, breaking the spell.

"Uh, yeah, right," Mark muttered. He turned quickly and stumbled off the stage, back into the seats. What was going on? Usually when he fooled around with someone, he hoped he'd never see them again.

But the fact was, he and Laura were starting to become friends, and he kind of looked forward to hanging out with her. And that meant he couldn't hook up with her because that was the last thing you did with a friend. Besides, she had Ted, who obviously made her totally happy. So, it was simple: He just had to find a way to stop fantasizing about Laura Whitman.

Yeah, Mark thought, watching her move gracefully across the stage, *real simple.*

Laura threw herself down on the living-room sofa and sighed. Play rehearsal had run late today—she'd just gotten home, and it was almost dinnertime. She let her eyes close, trying to relax as she ran through some of her lines in her head.

She pictured her love scene with Ted, smiling as she imagined it. He stood so close to her, his deep blue eyes boring into hers, that dimple in his cheek—

Mark! Laura's eyes popped open as she realized the truth. *I'm thinking of Mark, not Ted!*

A blush spread over her cheeks as she remembered Mark showing her how to stand during rehearsal. She could still almost feel the warmth of his hands on her arms.

"This has got to stop," she muttered, dragging herself up from the couch. "Mark is only good as a friend. Ted's who I should be fantasizing about."

She decided to go upstairs and check the answering machine for messages—that should take her mind off these embarrassing memories. She went into her parents' room and pushed play on the machine, barely listening as some friend of her dad's rambled on. *I wonder if Mark felt as awkward as I did when he had to touch me today,* she thought.

"Hello, Mr. and Mrs. Whitman, this is Mr. Seward calling." Laura snapped to attention. Mr. Seward was the junior-high-school principal. "I'd like to talk to you about your daughter Julie. Could you please call me back?"

Laura stared at the machine. Mr. Seward wanted

to talk to her parents? That was big. She ran down the hall to her sister's room and burst in, waking her up.

"What's wrong with you?" Julie asked. "I was sleeping!"

"You're always sleeping," Laura muttered. "Listen, what's going on with you at school?"

Julie sat up, looking uncomfortable. "What do you mean?" she asked.

"Mr. Seward left a message on the machine for Mom and Dad."

Julie's green eyes widened. "Oh my God, Laura, please, we have to erase it!"

Laura shook her head. "Jules, he'll just call back—he's not a total idiot." She sat down next to Julie on her bed, pushing aside the dark blue bedspread. "Come on," she started softly, "tell me what's wrong."

Julie looked down at the comforter. "He's probably calling because I haven't been doing all my homework lately," she admitted. "Or paying attention in class. Or going to all my classes. I've kind of skipped a couple."

"What?" Laura cried. She took a deep breath, telling herself to calm down. "Why on earth would you be messing up like this?"

"I don't know, okay?" A tear trickled down Julie's cheek. "I just feel so weird lately, so . . . *emotional* about everything. I try to concentrate on things, but I can't. All I want to do is sleep."

Laura hated to see her little sister looking so sad, but

she still didn't understand what was wrong. Something must have happened to make Julie so upset.

"Okay, I know a new school year is overwhelming," she began, "but you seem to be overreacting." Then she had a thought. "Maybe your problem is how much you've been sleeping. Maybe you're all sluggish because you need to wake up—you know, exercise or something like that."

Julie didn't look convinced. "I don't feel like I have the energy."

Laura stood up and started to pace back and forth, taking in the room. Everything looked normal enough. There were the pictures of Julie's friends above her desk, the same old posters of singers like Tori Amos and Sarah McLachlan. Laura stopped in place and turned back to face her sister. Julie's *the only thing that's different in here,* she thought.

"Look," she said, locking eyes with her sister. "Tell me the truth—what is it that's got you so freaked out?"

"Aren't you listening to me?" Julie asked in an anguished voice. "I told you over and over—there *isn't* anything."

Laura sighed in frustration. Why couldn't Julie just pull herself together and deal?

"Julie, you know I love you and I'd do anything for you, but right now I don't know what to say. When Mom and Dad hear about —"

"Wait, no!" Julie burst out. "This is between me and you, Laura. Please, for me, don't say anything about what I told you," she pleaded.

"What are you going to tell them after they talk to Mr. Seward?"

Julie paused, then shook her head. "I don't know—I'll make something up. And I'll start going to my classes and doing my work. Really, Laura, I will. I promise."

Laura hated the idea of keeping anything from her parents—her family didn't do secrets. But she knew this would just make them worry, which she didn't want either. And it was hard to say no to Julie.

"All right, here's the deal," Laura said. "I won't tell them how upset you are if you swear that you'll really get your act together in school *and* you'll tell me if anything else like this happens with you again. Okay?"

Julie nodded, her face brightening. "I promise I'll be better. Thank you!" She leaned over and hugged Laura tightly.

"You don't have to thank me," Laura told her. "That's what families are for."

"He shoots, and . . ." The ball flew out of Doug's hands and sank into the net with a familiar *whoosh*. "He scores!" Doug went after the basketball and dribbled it around the pavement, tossing it to Mark. "Your ball," he told him.

After school Mark had felt the need to get out his frustration in a way that he'd known writing wouldn't satisfy, so he'd driven over to Doug's house for some one-on-one in the driveway.

Mark caught the ball, dribbled, then moved up to the net to take a shot. The ball left his hands and whacked the board hard before flying back at him.

Doug grabbed the rebound, laughing. "What's with you, Adams?" he mocked. "It's not like you to miss an easy free throw." Doug threw the ball back up and watched as he made another basket. "So, what's up?" he asked.

Mark shrugged, sitting down on the curb. "I don't know," he said. "Maybe I'm stressed about this screenplay I've been working on. I can't come up with anything good."

Doug dropped down next to him, wiping sweat off his face. "You're letting a writing project get you this bent?"

Mark focused on his sneakers. "Yeah, I guess," he answered. "I don't know." The last thing he was in the mood for was an introspective conversation. "Come on," he said, forcing a grin and standing up. "I'm not letting you off that easy."

Mark grabbed the ball from Doug's hand, dribbling over to the hoop. But just as he was about to shoot, another image flashed through his mind—the look on Laura's face when he'd touched her at rehearsal. He threw the ball up angrily, missing the backboard completely this time.

"Air ball," Doug sang out from behind him.

Mark turned around. "Basketball's a stupid game anyway," he muttered.

Doug shook his head. "It's your favorite sport, freak."

"*You're* the freak."

Doug just rolled his eyes. "Adams, I'm getting worried about you. You're wound up so tight these past few days. What's the deal?" His face turned serious. "It's not your mom, is it?"

"My mom?" The question took Mark by surprise, and he looked down at the ground, feeling guilty for keeping something from one of his best friends, someone who knew him so well.

"Jeez, man, it is, isn't it?" Doug walked closer to Mark, the ball tucked under his elbow. "What happened?"

"No, no, my mom's fine." Mark grimaced. "Well, as fine as she ever is, at least."

"Then what is it?" Doug demanded.

Mark shook his head. "It's nothing, okay? God, you're like my girlfriend or something!"

They both cracked up as soon as the words came out of Mark's mouth.

"Sorry, dude," Doug said, still snickering. "But you're not my type. I prefer blondes."

Hmmm. Blondes. Mark actually preferred brunettes. He loved the color of Laura's hair—deep brown. *You must chill,* Mark yelled inwardly. Laura's hair was irrelevant to the situation. To *all* situations.

"You know, that gives me an idea," Doug said with a mysterious twinkle in his eye. "I think I know what's bugging you, man." He sat back down on the curb, setting the ball on the ground.

Mark froze. Could Doug possibly have found

out the truth somehow? No, there was no way. Besides, Doug kept secrets about as well as Mark was playing basketball today. He never would have held out this long if he knew that Mark had hooked up with Laura. Mark relaxed, dropping down on the cement in front of Doug, his legs stretched out in front of him. "What have you realized, O Wise One?" he kidded.

Doug smiled. "What you need, my friend, is a girl. A cutie. A hottie. A—"

"I get the picture," Mark cut him off. Cuties and hotties were *not* what he wanted to be thinking about.

"I was right!" Doug announced proudly. "You've been going through a dry spell lately, huh?" He shook his head sympathetically.

"Look," Mark teased, "just because all it takes to make you happy is a well-endowed girl in a sweater that's two sizes too small—"

"Actually," Doug interrupted, "I'm really a leg man. Not that I can't appreciate the fine beauty of an outgrown shirt, but—"

"You're awful," Mark told him, laughing. He reached out to grab the basketball, which had been slowly rolling away from them, and pretended to throw it at Doug but caught it right away.

Doug jerked back his head. "What are you, the sensitivity police or something? You're throwing stones from a seriously glass house here."

Mark was about to snap at his friend when it sank in that maybe Doug's idea wasn't all wrong.

Maybe a meaningless hookup with a girl he knew he could forget about in a second would be the way to distract himself from these annoying Laura fantasies. God, the Laura Fantasies—it sounded like a stupid romance saga.

"Mark? You there?"

"Huh? Oh, yeah. Just thinking about the, uh, screenplay scene, you know." Mark kicked the ball back and forth between his feet.

"Yeah, whatever. Are you ready to get back into the game?" Doug jumped up, scooping the ball away from Mark at the same time.

Mark stood up, brushing dirt off the back of his jeans. "I'm ready."

Getting back into the game is exactly *what I need,* he thought. And he knew it wouldn't be too hard to find a girl if he just looked around a little. In no time he'd find one who'd turn his night with Laura into a distant, meaningless memory—just like all the rest.

EIGHT

"WHAT DO YOU think of these?" Laura held up a package of brightly colored crepe paper for Mark to look at.

He scrunched up his face. "Too loud."

Laura groaned. "They're better than the black streamers you wanted," she pointed out. They'd been in The Party Store at the mall for almost an hour, trying to find decorations they could agree on. Laura was convinced that Mark had somehow gotten the impression that Rosita's party was going to have a hip funeral theme or something. He was just so dark.

"Okay, you know what we need to do?" Mark said, taking the package out of her hands and placing it back on the shelf. "We need to ignore our own totally different tastes and think about what Rosi would want."

Laura pouted. "I was thinking of Rosi," she said defensively.

"Really? What about those pink plastic flowers you thought would be just *perfect?*" Mark raised his eyebrows, a small smile on his lips.

Laura smiled back guiltily. "Okay, maybe those weren't her style exactly," she admitted. "But who are you to talk? What about the movie marquee that you just *knew* would make the party?"

"It would have!" Mark protested. "But . . . I guess it's possible that Rosita might not have loved it completely."

Laura grinned at Mark, and he returned the smile. Then they both burst out laughing.

"We're a mess," Laura said. "How can two people as stubborn as we are do this together?"

Mark placed his hands on her shoulders, looking her in the eye. "Laura Whitman, we have a mission here," he said in a mock-serious tone. "Our job is to get inside our friend Rosita's head and figure out what would make *her* happy."

Laura nodded. "All right, Captain. Let's begin," she said, imitating Mark's military voice.

They spent the next fifteen minutes looking around the store. Laura forced herself not to pick up all the items she would want if this were her party. Then they finally came up with decorations that they agreed would please Rosita and brought them all over to the register.

As they walked out of the store, Laura wondered what they'd do next. Would Mark just take her right home? She hoped not—she was having a blast hanging out with him. She never had so much fun just talking to anyone except Rosita.

"So, do you want to walk around a little?" Mark asked her, shifting the bags from his left hand to his right.

"Yeah, sure," Laura replied. "There's nothing like a Jersey mall for a good adventure, right?"

Mark laughed, navigating his way around a group of screaming ten-year-olds. "Kevin Smith thought it was worth a whole movie."

"You mean *Mall Rats*?" Laura asked, sniffing. "That was so stupid."

"Yeah, it was," Mark agreed. "Hey, wait, you actually knew a *director* I was talking about. I'm impressed."

Laura tossed back her ponytail proudly. "Of course I know him," she said. "He made that *Chasing Amy* movie that Ben Affleck was in."

Mark rolled his eyes but smiled. "Oh, well, at least you know who he is." He paused. "And hey, we actually agreed on something too."

"That's a first," Laura joked. "Quick, find something we can argue about."

"Um, okay . . . Let's see . . . actors versus directors?"

"Come on, Mark, we've done that one already."

Mark stopped walking, pretending to look scared. "Well, we better come up with something fast before this turns into *The Twilight Zone* and we both melt into green blobs of goo."

"Ew!" Laura squealed. Then she noticed the Warner Brothers store across from where they were standing. "Hey, I know you're going to make fun of me, but I have to go in there," she said, pointing.

"Why would I tease you for that?" Mark asked. "I love that place."

"You do?" Laura asked, waiting for him to back up his remark with some sort of snide comment. There was no way Mr. Cynical could really like something as silly as the Warner Brothers store.

"Yeah. How can you not love Animaniacs? Besides, you do know that Steven Spielberg produces the show, right?"

Laura nodded. "I watch it all the time." She narrowed her eyes, studying him. "What about Tweety? And Taz? Are they cool enough for you?"

Mark's face turned a slight pinkish color. Laura would've even considered it a blush if she'd thought that was possible for a guy who didn't seem capable of feeling ashamed of *anything*. "I love Taz," he confessed weakly.

"Come on, then, let's go in!" Laura grabbed Mark's arm and pulled him into the store.

"Look at that!" she exclaimed once they were inside. "They put in new games. Oh, we have to go in the little ship back there, okay?" She turned to Mark with a pleading expression and pointed to Marvin the Martian's spaceship.

"Uh, Laura, that's for little kids—like young Johnny over there," Mark said, pointing to a boy who looked about three and had just emerged from the giant toy.

Laura laughed. "We can fit. It won't kill you to

have a good time, Mark." She leaned closer to him and whispered, "I won't tell anyone that I saw you enjoying yourself doing something totally not dark and depressing, okay?"

Mark gave her a playful shove. "Be quiet." Then with a wide grin he marched over to the spaceship and squeezed himself inside. Laura hurried over behind him, trying to keep from laughing out loud at the sight of Mr. Cool all crouched up in front of a fake control panel with bright, flashing lights. "You'd better get in here too," he warned her.

Laura obeyed, climbing in next to him. "What do you think this does?" she asked, pointing to a round, red button. She reached out to push it, and Mark grabbed her hand.

"No!" he cried. "That would launch the missiles to destroy Earth."

Laura nodded solemnly. "Of course. So what's our next move, Captain?"

Mark surveyed the panel quickly. "I think it's clear that our best choice would be the yellow triangle," he declared. "Go for it."

As she leaned over Mark to hit the button, her hand grazed his leg, and Laura suddenly felt extremely aware of how close they were to each other. She was practically sitting on his lap, and their legs were smooshed together. And now that she thought about it, it was really hot in here. Too hot.

"Maybe we should let the kids have a chance," Laura mumbled, avoiding Mark's gaze. She didn't think she could handle staring into those blue eyes, not with the way her pulse was racing. And the way she was sweating! It was like there was no air in that thing. "I mean, aren't you warm?" Laura pushed her way out.

Mark followed her, taking a little longer to extricate his legs. "I have a sneaking suspicion that ship wasn't made for people my size," he commented, smiling.

Laura laughed, still trying to regain her sense of balance. Her heart was beating *very* fast. She had to get control of herself—which meant she had to *not* focus on his face.

They sat down on a bench decorated with Tiny Toon characters, next to a giant Superman statue. Laura took a deep breath, wondering why being close to Mark had affected her so much. After all, he was just a friend, and she had no desire to repeat their one night of pure stupidity on her part. So then why was she starting to feel like there really *was* something else between them? Laura edged away from Mark, toward the opposite end of the bench.

"What's your take on the old debate—you know, who's the cooler superhero, Superman or Batman?" Mark asked, inspecting the figure next to him.

"Obviously Superman," Laura stated, relieved to distract herself with silly conversation. "He's the one who can see through walls, move at the speed of light, all that stuff. I mean, Batman is fine and all, but he's just a guy dressed up in a fancy outfit."

Mark sighed. "That's exactly what makes Batman better," he argued. "Anyone who has the powers of Superman could run around and save the world. But Batman's an ordinary guy who *made* himself into a superhero. Plus he's got the whole haunted-past-and-troubled-soul thing. Much more interesting than squeaky-clean Supe here."

"Well, sure, anyone with superpowers could help people out," Laura agreed. "But did you ever think that he could just as easily not? You have to give Superman credit for *choosing* to do good with his powers. And who cares about Batman's troubled soul? That doesn't necessarily make him more intriguing."

"Please," Mark replied, shaking his head. "Superman might make a great date to bring home to Mom. But be honest—if you could choose to spend a night with him or with Batman, who do you think would show you a better time? Isn't all that mystery of the Bat-dude pretty sexy?"

Laura thought about this for a moment, playing with the ends of her ponytail. Why did she suddenly feel like they were talking about something deeper than comic-book characters? "Maybe hanging with Batman would be exciting," Laura told him, surprised to hear an edge in her own voice. Where was that anger coming from? "But he wouldn't be reliable," she continued, her voice rising. "Superman seems like someone who would keep his promises. With Batman you never know what the deal is. He's always showing up and then disappearing into the night. You can't trust him or know what to expect next." A few people turned to stare at them, and Laura realized that her voice had gotten a bit loud. Her cheeks flushing, she cut herself off and leaned back on the bench.

"All right. Enough of that debate." Mark ran a hand through his hair. "Did you want to look at anything else before we go?"

Laura glanced around. "What's that?" she asked, pointing to an interesting-looking booth.

Mark shrugged. "Let's check it out." They got up and walked closer, and Laura saw that it was a photo booth where you could get your picture taken with a Warner Brothers character in the background.

"That's so cool," she said when she figured it out. "What are the choices?"

They both scanned the images, then looked up at each other at the same moment.

"We have to do it," Mark said.

"It's too perfect," Laura agreed. "That is, if you're looking at the one I am."

Mark put his finger on the picture of Pinky and the Brain, and Laura smiled. "You got it," she told him. She knew he had pegged her as the carefree and silly Pinky just as quickly as she'd seen him as the darker, overly serious Brain.

They put their money in and posed, with

Laura's head on Pinky's body and Mark's on the Brain's. Two big sheets of photos came out, and they each took one to keep.

"I'm hungry," Mark announced when they were finished laughing at the pictures.

"Me too. Want to get some pizza?"

"Sounds good."

They left the Warner Brothers store and headed in the direction of the food court. Tony's Slice had a short line when they got there, and it wasn't long before they were sitting down at a table with their food.

Mark scarfed down his first slice in seconds. Laura smiled as she watched him, marveling at the way he, like most guys, could eat so fast. He paused before starting in on his second, leaning over the table toward her. "Check out the guy in line at Chicken Tender," he stage-whispered.

Laura turned to see who he meant and giggled when she spotted him—some scrawny man arguing with the poor kid behind the counter, flapping his arms around and looking very much like a chicken himself.

"What's his problem?" she asked Mark, shaking her head.

"Shhh, listen," he instructed.

Laura put down her pizza and tried to hear what the man was yelling about. His voice got louder, and she could finally make out that his large soda had actually *not* been filled all the way to the top and when you divided the price of the beverage by the amount he had decided was missing, it became obvious that he was owed exactly twenty-three cents.

"He has no life," Laura pronounced, taking a sip of her diet Coke.

"Seriously," Mark said. "He's one of those types who tries to use five of the same coupon at the supermarket—so that he can get his toilet paper for free."

Laura started laughing again, pushing her soda away from her so that she wouldn't choke. "And he hasn't had a date since that time a few years ago when he brought a calculator and made sure the woman paid the correct percent of tax and tip for her dinner."

Mark smiled, glancing around the food court. "Okay, what about that woman?" he asked, quickly jerking his head to the left to point her out. "Blue dress. Huge shopping bags. What's her story?"

"Hmmm." Laura took a peek at the woman, then paused to think. "Okay," she said, leaning in to Mark. "She just found out her husband cheated on her, so she's maxing out his credit cards before she leaves him."

Mark shook his head. "Man, women are harsh."

"Hey," Laura argued. "The guy cheated on her with another woman! What do you expect Ms. Blue Dress to do, give him a big hug and say thank you?"

Mark's blue eyes twinkled. Boy, did Laura love those eyes. And that dimple . . . She was having so much fun with him. More fun than she'd had in a while. Was it possible that she'd been wrong? *Maybe we could be a*—

"Okay, point taken," Mark said, interrupting her thoughts. "Who's next?"

Trying to ignore the sudden rapid beating of her heart, Laura took in the crowd behind Mark. She couldn't let him know how she was feeling. *But maybe if we spent more time like this together*—

"Laura? This isn't a competition. There has to be someone worthy of our comments over there," Mark teased.

"Of course," Laura said, blood rushing to her cheeks. *Stop thinking. Just pick someone. Anyone.* She spotted a tall, beautiful girl with long, auburn hair walking in their direction. "Girl our age, tall, red hair," she told Mark. "Definitely here to pick out the right nail polish for her date tonight."

Mark smirked. "I know the type."

"Wait, she's headed this way—check her out and see what you think. Is she here for the nail polish or the lipstick?"

Mark chuckled, turning slightly to look just as the redheaded girl was almost at their table. But when the girl saw Mark, she stopped walking and smiled.

Wait—did they know each other?

"Hey, Mark!" She bounced over to him, and Laura swallowed—hard.

Mark stood and gave her a hug. Laura felt her entire body clench. No doubt this was one of

Mark's many conquests. *You're one of his conquests,* Laura reminded herself, suddenly feeling ill.

"Debi, what's up?" he asked the redhead once they'd pulled apart. His eyes moved up and down her body, and Laura felt even more nauseous. How could she be so stupid? How could she even think for a second that there'd be a chance for her and Mark? How could she *want* a chance with him?

"You look great," he was saying to Debi.

Laura folded her arms against her chest, trying to stay calm. *You don't want Mark anyway,* she told herself. *You just had a moment of temporary insanity. You have Ted—a guy you're crazy about. A guy you know you can trust.*

"Your hair is so long!" Debi squealed, reaching out to touch it.

Mark bent his head closer to her hands, smiling. "Well, it's been a while since we, uh . . ." He stopped, looking at her, his eyes twinkling mischievously.

Ugh, Laura thought. *Please spare me.*

Debi swatted his shoulder playfully. "You're still a brat, aren't you?" she teased.

You're still a brat, Laura mimicked in her head, trying not to groan.

"It's great to see you, Mark, but I have to get some stuff done, 'kay?"

Mark nodded. "Sure, go ahead. Take care, Deb."

"You too." With a last little wave Debi walked

away, leaving Laura with an intense need to get out of the mall and as far away from Mark as possible. And a sudden desire to call Ted.

"So, what were we saying?" Mark asked her distractedly, still staring after Debi.

"Maybe we should go," Laura told Mark tightly.

He looked at her questioningly. "Now?"

"Yes. I have a lot of things to do at home."

"Okay." He shrugged.

They threw out their trash and walked toward the mall exit, Laura fighting hard not to betray any of her emotions. The last thing she wanted was for Mark to actually think she was jealous. And she wasn't, really. Why would she want Mark, a guy who clearly couldn't focus on any one girl or keep any promises, when she had Ted, a guy who was worlds more right for her? This whole experience was just one more sign of how true that was. Mark might be fun to have as a friend, but that was all.

Yep, that's definitely what I want, she told herself as Mark pushed open the glass door. *Ted as a boyfriend, Mark as a friend. A good friend. A good friend with beautiful eyes and—a good friend, that's all.*

NINE

SPENDING YOUR SATURDAY night working at Video World had to be listed somewhere in a book titled *101 Ways to Know If You're a Total Loser*. At least, that's how it seemed to Mark as he stood behind the counter, sorting returned movies.

It'll make a good quote someday when Entertainment Weekly is interviewing me after my first big hit, he thought. *"Yeah, when I was in high school, I used to spend my weekends working in the video store. Now I can't even go to a video store without being mobbed by all my fans."*

He heard the sound of the door swinging open and reflexively turned his head to greet the customer. Maybe it would be Mike and Doug, showing up to put a dent in his boredom.

It wasn't Mike and Doug. Not even close.

Instead Laura and Ted were standing there, holding hands and smiling at each other. Mark felt a weird twisting in his stomach. Of course, Laura looked beautiful. At least she was wearing long pants tonight. Long, tight pants, however. He couldn't win.

"Hey, Adams," Ted said. "How's work?"

Mark hated the way guys like Ted loved to act all friendly to everyone, even people they barely knew. "Fine," Mark answered. He glanced at Laura, who gave him a small, not too sincere smile. He forced back a smile. She'd been weird with him the whole ride home from the mall yesterday, as if he'd upset her somehow, but he had no idea what he'd done.

Still, come to think of it, putting a little distance between him and Laura wouldn't be a bad thing. It would help him to stop thinking about what it was like when, well, when there was just about no distance between their bodies. . . .

"We're here to get a movie," Ted continued, draping his arm around Laura.

Gee, Mark was glad Ted had pointed that out since there was no way he *ever* would've figured it out on his own. "That's cool," Mark replied. Wasn't renting a movie a total make-out date? The thought made him strangely uneasy.

"Hey, man, maybe you could recommend something. Maybe a good horror movie?" Ted looked at Laura. "Does that sound okay?"

"Sure," Laura said quietly.

"Tell me one that's really scary," Ted said.

A really scary horror movie? Mark had heard

somewhere that horror flicks were supposed to be a total turn-on for people. And Laura was his friend. He didn't want some guy putting his hands all over his *friend*. . . .

"You know what?" Mark said, picking up a random video that had just been returned and holding it out to Ted. "This new comedy, *Stealing Grace*, just came out on video. It's supposed to be hilarious." *And totally not sexy*, Mark thought. "Why don't you guys try it?"

Ted shrugged. "Okay, if you say so."

Just then the door opened again, and Amanda London and Stacey Muzin walked into the store. Amanda was wearing a supershort skirt that drew Mark's eyes right to her long, tan legs.

"This is so funny!" Amanda squealed when she saw all of them. "It's like an *Only Today* rehearsal. At least of the important people." She giggled, staring straight at Mark.

Mark smiled back. "Hey, Amanda," he said, leaning his elbow on the counter. She'd been flirting with him a fair amount in school, and he had to admit she wasn't at all hard on the eyes. "Can I help you pick out a movie?"

"I think we should get going," Laura said to Ted, tugging on his arm.

"Yeah. We'll try *Stealing Grace*," Ted said. He handed over his membership card, and Mark rang up the rental. "Have fun," he told them as they went around to the exit door. Laura turned back to look at him with a funny expression, her face all twisted up. Then she swung back around and walked out of the store with Ted.

"Those two were in a hurry to be alone," Amanda commented. "I never thought Ted would find someone as perfect for him as Emily, but I guess I was wrong."

"Yeah," Mark mumbled, trying to ignore the bad taste in his mouth.

Amanda smiled, leaning over the counter toward him. Then she glanced quickly at Stacey. "Stace, why don't you go pick out a movie?" Stacey nodded and walked over to the new-release aisle.

"It must get really dull here, huh?"

Mark groaned. "Extremely."

Amanda leaned in even closer. She was wearing some kind of incredibly sexy perfume. "I *hate* being bored," she whispered.

Mark shifted uncomfortably. Oh, man. It wasn't right to do this to a guy when he was at work. Still, he found himself moving nearer to Amanda. "So do I."

Stacey reappeared. "Amanda? I found something."

"That was fast," Amanda said in an irritated voice. Mark couldn't help smiling.

Stacey didn't seem to notice Amanda's frustration. "Yeah, well, I saw this right away." She waved the movie around in her hand. "Come on, we have to meet Jill soon."

Amanda sighed. "Yeah, okay." She looked back at Mark. "See you soon?"

Mark grinned. "Definitely," he told her. The

two girls paid for the movie and left, and Mark went back to sorting the returned videos.

Clearly Amanda was making herself available to him. And he'd have to be an idiot not to go for her—she was sexy, and she was . . . well, she was sexy. Plus she was the perfect opportunity to begin plan Back in the Game.

Maybe next week I'll ask her out, Mark thought as he rewound a tape. *She seems like the perfect, no-strings-attached way to get my mind off . . . other people.*

Laura shifted around on the sofa, wondering why she was having so much trouble getting comfortable. Ever since she and Ted had left Video World, she'd felt agitated.

"That Adams *is* kind of weird," Ted said as he put the tape in the VCR. "I can see why you don't like him much."

Laura played with the fringe on the Legums' sofa pillows. She wasn't sure what to say—she'd always made such a point of disliking Mark. But now that they were sort of friends, she felt like she should defend him or something.

"Didn't you say you two had a mutual friend?" Ted asked.

"Yes, my friend Rosita."

"She's Dennis Kerzner's girlfriend, right?"

"Exactly," Laura told him.

"We should all go out together sometime," he said. "Dennis seems cool."

113

Laura's heart jumped. Double dating with Rosita had always been her dream, and Ted had been the one to suggest it! It was like they were totally in sync. Someone like *Mark,* on the other hand, would probably think double dates were lame.

Then Laura had another equally exciting thought: If Ted was talking about the future like that, she had to mean something to him, right?

Ted settled onto the couch next to her. "Let's see what kind of taste Adams has in movies," he said, hitting play on the remote.

Why did he have to mention Mark again? Laura immediately got a mental picture of Mark flirting with Amanda in the video store. And Mark flirting with that redhead at the mall. And with Rosi's friend Abby in school . . .

"Hey, what are you daydreaming about?" Ted's voice broke into her thoughts.

I can't believe I'm wasting my time thinking about Mark Adams when I'm here with a great guy, Laura thought, disgusted with herself. "You," she lied.

Ted leaned over to kiss her. She closed her eyes and put her arms around his neck, pulling him to her. He kissed her deeply, and she relaxed. Ted had that effect on her—he made her feel secure. It was nothing like that weird, nervous thing that she'd felt in her stomach when she'd been at the mall with Mark.

After all, that was what boyfriends were for—making you feel safe.

TEN

"HEY, WHAT'S UP?" Rosita slid into the seat next to Mark, flashing him a smile. It was Monday morning, and Mark was early for creative writing.

"Nothing much. What about you?" Mark reached into his backpack to pull out his notebook.

Rosita shrugged. "The usual. Did you come up with a screenplay scene idea? It's due at the end of next week."

Mark groaned. "Don't remind me."

"Hi, Mark!" Amanda London called from the doorway to the classroom.

He swung around in his seat to wave at her. "Hey, Amanda," he called back. "Cool skirt."

Behind him Rosita snorted, but he kept smiling at Amanda as if he hadn't heard it.

Amanda giggled. "Thanks. See you at rehearsal." She headed off down the hall.

Mark turned back to Rosita. "You never compliment *me* on my outfits," she teased, pouting.

He swatted her arm playfully. "Oh, leave me alone. There's no harm in flirting with a cute girl."

"Unless she thinks you mean what you say," Rosita said, more seriously. "And unless she's someone I care about and don't want you to hurt."

Mark winced. "Rosi, I already told you how sorry I am about the whole Laura thing. I messed up, but it's history now, so can we drop it? I mean, your friend is blissfully happy with that Legum dope anyway, so—"

"He's not a dope!" Rosita interjected. She paused, then continued, "I mean, he wouldn't be *my* first choice, but he's a very talented actor, which means a lot to Laura. Besides, he treats her well, from what she tells me."

"Good," Mark responded stiffly. "So obviously what happened between Laura and me didn't matter at all to her. She's with Ted, and they're happy together."

"Yeah. They're perfect for each other," Rosita said, watching him with a strange look on her face.

See? Mark thought. *If Ted really is perfect for Laura, that just proves how wrong I am for her.* Not that he had to prove to himself he was wrong for Laura anyway. He'd known that from the start. And she was all wrong for him too. It was just like he'd told himself after Laura had kissed him at that

116

party—hooking up with him had been a tiny bump of the unexpected in Laura's little life plan, but she had moved on. She had rebelled for that one night, and now she was back with Ted, where she belonged.

"Okay, everyone, time to get started." Mark looked up and saw that Mr. Greif had come in and set himself up at the front of the classroom.

"Today I'd like to talk about clichés," Mr. Greif began, leaning back against his desk. "There are many ways that clichés can manifest themselves. To write well, it's necessary to avoid them all."

The only thing I need to avoid right now is thinking about Laura Whitman, Mark told himself, stretching his legs out in front of him.

Mark peeled off his sweater and tossed it over to the side of the stage. Autumn in New Jersey had very confusing weather. This morning it had been chilly, but now that he was moving all this heavy furniture around for rehearsal, he was glad he'd worn a T-shirt underneath. Of course, the stage lights made it especially hot. "Is this good?" he asked Ms. Goldstein, hoping she'd be happy with his placement of the couch.

She scrunched up her face, cupping her chin in her hand. "A little to the left, actually, Mark. Thanks a lot."

Mark paused, wondering again why getting into this whole play thing had seemed like such a great idea. Apparently Ms. Goldstein had decided that manual labor was part of his job since her stage manager was a girl who freaked out if she had to lift a costume.

When he finished moving props around, Mark jumped off the stage. He collapsed into a seat in the auditorium before he realized that Laura and Ted were sitting right behind him.

"Oh, hey," he said. "How was the movie the other night?"

Ted nodded. "It was pretty funny. Thanks for the rec, buddy."

"Anytime," Mark responded, attempting to sound friendly. He looked at Laura. "What did you think? You liked it too?"

"Yeah, I did."

Well, that sure was a descriptive response. Mark stared at her for a moment as she played with the ends of her hair. Why was it that she'd barely looked him in the eye the past few days?

"Um, maybe we should go backstage and run through our lines," Ted said to Laura. Laura gave Mark a small smile, then got up and followed Ted.

Mark settled into his seat and tried to focus on preparing for the scenes they were going to rehearse that day. He imagined the actors' placements and movements, jotting down ideas on a little notepad. But he couldn't stop thinking about the way Laura looked with Ted, so happy. What did she see in that walking Ken doll?

What do I care? It's not like I need her or anything.

"Hey, Mark!" a cheerful female voice greeted him, pulling him out of his thoughts.

Mark turned to see Amanda standing behind him. *Perfect timing,* he thought. If he didn't stop thinking about Laura soon, he'd go crazy.

"Amanda, hey. What's up?" he asked. "Have a seat."

Amanda's face lit up, her bright blue eyes sparkling, and she quickly walked around to join him. "What are you working on?" she asked, glancing at his notepad.

"Just stage directions and stuff," he said. "Nothing as interesting as talking to you."

She smiled. "Thanks. I like talking to you too."

Mark felt better than he had in weeks. Since the night he kissed Laura, in fact. All he'd needed was another girl to fool around with. "Well, maybe we should hang out sometime so that we can . . . *talk* some more."

"Sounds good," Amanda practically purred.

"How about this weekend?" he asked. "Friday night?"

Amanda giggled. "That works for me."

Doug was right, Mark decided, leaning back into his seat. *Once I'm back out there, hanging with other girls, I'll loosen up fast and stop thinking about Laura. And I'll have fun in the process.*

Laura fumbled with the lock to her front door, getting increasingly angry as the key just wouldn't fit in the right way. "What's the matter with this

119

thing?" she muttered in frustration. Finally it turned, and she shoved her body against the door, even though it always opened easily. Once she was inside the house, she threw her backpack on the floor and dropped down onto the couch, putting her head in her hands.

Why am I letting this get to me? she wondered miserably. *Why does it drive me crazy to watch Mark with Amanda when I have Ted and I'm so happy with him?*

Ever since play rehearsal, when she'd seen Amanda and Mark all over each other, she had been in a terrible mood. The bus ride home had seemed to last a hundred years, every bump and jolt punctuating her bad attitude.

The phone rang. With a groan Laura went into the den to answer it.

"Hello?"

"Hi, Laura?" Ted's warm voice filled Laura with the usual sense of security. And that kind of security was just what she needed at the moment.

"Yeah, hey, Ted." She sat down on the sofa, twirling the phone cord between her fingers.

"So, what's going on with you?" he asked.

"Same old stuff. What about you?"

"I've been working on my lines." He sighed. "I wish Ms. Goldstein hadn't decided to do such a complicated play, you know?"

"Actually, I'm kind of happy she chose *Only Today*," Laura admitted. "I mean, at least we're not doing *Oklahoma* for the fiftieth time or something."

"But I don't even get so much of what's going on. Do you?"

Laura paused. The meaning behind this play had always been fairly clear to her. "Um, yeah," she finally answered. "It's sort of about the different ways people see time and how the past can mean all kinds of things to everyone."

"Whatever," Ted said, sounding annoyed. "Why can't the characters just say that instead of being all symbolic about it?"

That was what Laura loved about *Only Today*. The play didn't spell everything out on the surface for the audience. Instead it showed more of what was happening inside the characters' heads, asking the audience to come to their own conclusions. It was kind of upsetting that Ted didn't see it that way at all. So far they'd always agreed on everything. But then again, they'd never really talked much about anything serious.

"I guess *I* like it because I'm a language person and all," Laura offered.

"Huh? What do you mean?"

Laura bit her lip. It was her fault that he didn't know this about her—she hadn't been very good at opening up with him on their first few dates. Now was her chance. "Well, I love learning other languages. And trying to interpret a play is a lot like trying to translate something—it's all about seeing how different people interpret the same words." She stopped, feeling awkward, since Ted was silent on the other end. "But I guess I can see how that wouldn't be very exciting for everyone," she added quickly.

"All I know is that trying to memorize these crazy lines isn't exciting at all," Ted said, sounding frustrated. Then he let out another sigh. "Anyway, I wanted to see if you're free Friday night," he continued in a more upbeat tone. "I thought maybe we could go somewhere nice for dinner. I could make reservations."

"Sure," Laura replied. "That sounds great." Dinner at a fancy restaurant was only her total dream come true. But for some reason, her heart didn't start to race at his words as it usually did. In fact, she almost felt bored by the idea of dinner with nothing really to talk about.

"Cool. We'll figure out the details later, okay? I should go get some work done."

"Sure. Bye, Ted." Laura hung up the phone, lying back on the couch to think.

This had been their first attempt at an actual semideep conversation—and it had been super-awkward. What did that mean? She was happy when she was with Ted, definitely. She loved knowing that he liked her, she loved how he treated her, but . . . well, she'd always thought that when she fell in love for the first time, she'd be ecstatic. And she wasn't. At first every moment with Ted had thrilled her. But that wasn't exactly true anymore.

She'd read somewhere that love felt like floating on clouds made of cotton candy. So where was all the pink fluff?

I'm making too much of this, Laura reasoned, sitting up. *This was the first time things have ever been awkward between us—that's going to happen sometimes. Ted was just in a weird mood, that's all.*

After all, she *knew* he was the right guy for her. How could he not be?

ELEVEN

"So, WHAT'S NEW on the Ted front?" Rosita took a big bite of her sandwich, a few shreds of lettuce falling out onto the table. She always brought her own lunches, ultrahealthy concoctions to prevent the heart disease she was convinced would strike her before she'd reached twenty.

Laura, on the other hand, trusted herself to the Park Hills High fare, which today consisted of chicken with rice and beans. On Thursdays they always served their "ethnic specials." She giggled. "What's in that one?" she asked, pointing to her friend's sandwich.

Rosita swallowed, then grinned. "Lettuce, sprouts, and tomato with mustard on a whole-wheat pita," she announced. "Actually pretty good. Want a taste?"

"I don't think so," Laura answered, wrinkling her nose. "I'll stick to the pseudo-Mexican blob from the cafeteria." She stuck a forkful of rice in her mouth, trying to pretend it had flavor. "Anyway, about Ted," she resumed. "Things are really good. I mean, he's everything I've ever wanted. Totally reliable and dependable."

Rosita gave her a funny look. "You don't sound thrilled."

"What do you mean?" Laura asked, her cheeks burning. "Of course I am. How could I not be?"

"I don't know. It *sounds* like you two are perfect for each other, but I'm not sure you're doing this because you *like* Ted. I think it's some weird reaction to that thing with Mark."

"No," Laura stated firmly. "Ted is totally perfect. You were right all along. Mark was a major mistake, and Ted's the best thing for me."

Rosita put down her sandwich and fixed her with a doubtful gaze.

Laura laughed nervously. "Come on, Rosi, Ted's one of the most popular, best-looking, and nicest guys at Park Hills. I'm not exactly settling here."

Rosita nodded. "Point taken." She finished her veggie sandwich and sipped her juice. "So, if everything with you is peachy, can we move on to my life?"

Laura grinned. "Please do. Is something wrong?"

Rosita sighed. "Oh, nothing, except for the fact that my sixteenth birthday is quickly approaching and I have *zero* plans aside from a family dinner."

Laura smiled to herself, thinking how psyched

Rosi was going to be when she showed up at Laura's house and found the surprise party waiting for her. She and Mark had been doing well with the guest list—so far almost everyone they'd invited was planning to come.

"Well, I know this isn't anything too exciting, but I told my parents about your boyfriendless birthday, and my mom wants you to stop over that night for a little minicelebration with us and a couple of friends. Is that okay?"

Rosita smiled. "Your mom's so sweet. Yeah, that sounds nice. And I guess we can go catch a movie or something afterward," she added. "That is, unless you're going to be busy with your new man."

"Like I would ditch you for Ted. No way!" Laura said. Actually, she hadn't mentioned the surprise party to Ted yet. She felt weird about telling him that she was planning it with Mark. He thought she hated Mark. And somehow she couldn't face the idea of explaining why her opinion had changed.

Rosita's eyes moved to someone behind Laura, and her face brightened.

"Hello, ladies," Dennis greeted them, walking around Laura and sliding into the seat next to his girlfriend. "Look who I found eating all by himself." Laura turned to see who Dennis was referring to and found Mark standing behind her with his hands stuffed into his pockets. "You can sit down, you know," Dennis told Mark teasingly.

Mark glanced at Laura, then took a seat next to her.

Laura sat there silently, watching him open up his lunch bag, unsure of exactly how to act around him. She looked across the table at Rosita and noticed that her friend was studying her and Mark with a curious expression.

"What physics problem are you all attempting to solve here that I don't know about?" Dennis asked the three of them, smiling. Dennis might have been an academic genius, but he wasn't the quickest when it came to social situations. And since Rosita had promised not to tell him about Laura and Mark's kiss, he couldn't have any idea why things had suddenly become strange at the lunch table.

"The day I think about physics," Rosita began, "is the day that Laura shows up for school in baggy jeans and a sweatshirt with messy hair."

Dennis shrugged. "You guys just had funny looks on your faces, that's all."

"Ex*cuse* me," Rosita said, raising her eyebrows. "Where I come from, that's not how you compliment your girlfriend. Especially when she's been waiting for you to show up so that she can help you finish your English essay."

"Oops." Dennis's face went white. "I totally forgot about that." He shoved a forkful of food in his mouth, swallowing before he'd even seemed to chew. "We've got to go work on that, like, *now*." He turned to Laura and Mark. "Sorry, guys, do you mind if we bail?"

"Of course not," Laura responded, faking a cheery tone. The last thing she wanted was for

Mark to think she had some kind of problem with being around him. She didn't want him to think he affected her in *any* way—that would clearly just boost his ego. "Go ahead."

Rosita stood, stuffing her trash into her lunch bag. Dennis rose too, carrying his tray.

"I'll see you guys later, okay?" Rosita said, eyeing Laura and Mark thoughtfully. Then she turned, following Dennis out of the cafeteria.

Mark watched as Rosita and Dennis disappeared into the lunchroom crowd. He stuck some chips in his mouth, chewing loudly. At least it seemed loud to him since the table was suddenly very quiet. "Those two are something, aren't they?" he finally commented, breaking the silence. *Gee, Adams, what an exciting conversation starter.*

"Yes. They're pretty funny together," Laura answered, not quite meeting his eyes. She looked so good today, with her thick brown hair braided, a few wisps falling around her neck. *The plan is to not think about Laura like this,* Mark reminded himself. *I'm moving on, I'm letting go . . . and all those other John Wayne–type, lone-cowboy expressions.*

"So . . . how's your screenplay scene going?" Laura asked, moving the food around on her plate.

Mark sighed. "It's not." He shook his head. "I can't come up with any ideas for a good movie that haven't been done a million times. I mean, I think I could do a lot of them *better,*" he explained, grinning, "but I want to do something more original.

Something that really shows the truth about this world, the misery."

Laura rolled her eyes. "Every one of your ideas has to be dismal and depressing, doesn't it?" She pushed away her tray and smiled back at him. "Why do great movies always have to show people being miserable? Like *Braveheart*—remember that? Every bad thing possible had to happen to the guy. I mean, his family was killed, his wife was murdered. Please."

"Okay, *Braveheart* was a little extreme, but—"

"And then there's that old Brad Pitt one; what's it called?" Laura went on, cutting him off. "*Legends of the Fall.* Have you ever rented it? It's painful. By the end I was like, okay, so when is the house going to burn down and the whole world explode? It's like you're not supposed to root for the hero unless his life has been ridiculously hard. Why couldn't they have just killed the *Braveheart* guy's cat instead of absolutely everyone around him? He still would've been a great warrior."

Mark leaned his elbows on the table and stared intently at Laura. "Movies show all that sadness because that's what real life is like," he told her. "Would you really want to watch someone just be happy all the time, with no problems? That's not reality." Well, that was Laura's reality, he realized. Maybe that was her deal—she couldn't relate to misery because she'd never felt any.

"No, of course it's not," Laura agreed. "But life isn't as completely horrible as you seem to think, Mark."

How dare she act like he was the stupid one

when her life had been so easy? What did she know? "You haven't seen what I've seen," Mark responded, anger rising in his voice. "So you go on thinking life is all pretty and happy, but one day maybe you'll see that *my* life is closer to reality."

Laura's face softened, but when she continued, her voice was unyielding. "Don't you get it?" she asked. "Maybe you're the one who hasn't seen what *I've* seen. I grew up with two parents who love each other and my sister and me. My life is just as possible as yours. My reality is every bit as real as what you've lived through."

Mark blinked back at her, stunned into silence. He knew she had to be wrong, but something about what she had said was really hitting him. *It makes sense,* he thought, his mind reeling. He'd always been convinced that people with happy families were blind because they had never been abandoned, they'd never had to struggle for anything. But he'd never seen it from Laura's side—he'd never even considered that *he* was the one missing a perspective.

"I'm living proof that happy endings do happen," Laura said. "My family is open and honest and loving. It can happen."

Where was the catch here? Mark wondered, dumbfounded. Why wasn't he able to come up with something to say to her? Laura leaned toward him, waiting for a response, her eyes full of fire and intensity. She looked passionate and soft at the same time, so touchable, so kissable. . . .

"I—I don't know," Mark stammered. "I mean, I see what you're saying." He sat back a little, unnerved by the effect Laura's closeness was having on him. He still wanted her, and he hated it. And there was something else, something more . . . He just couldn't figure out what it was. "But I still disagree," he finished lamely. "Life in the real world is hard and unfair. When movies show that, they're being honest. Don't forget, *Braveheart* was based on a true story."

Laura sat back in her own chair, frowning. "You're impossible," she said, piling her trash on her tray. "For a second there it seemed like you were letting the truth sink in, but you just can't accept that anyone but you could be right about something, can you?"

"And you're any better?" Mark asked, raising his eyebrows. "You're so convinced that everything is exactly the way *you* think it is."

Laura stood up. "When you're working on your screenplay scene, think about what I'm saying. Maybe if you try to write something that's not just about how much life stinks, it'll give you some new ideas." She paused. "Don't they say that writers should write what they know?"

Mark nodded. "Yeah, so, see? What I know is *not* happy endings."

"But maybe if you write about your own experiences without turning it into a huge, melodramatic tragedy, you'll be able to come up with an original scene—like you wanted." She shrugged.

"Just a thought. Anyway, I'll see you later." She turned and walked off.

Mark leaned back in his chair, his brain a jumble of conflicting thoughts. No one had ever questioned him as much as Laura just had, and certainly no one had ever made *him* question himself at all. Usually when people found out about Mark's dad or heard about his overworked mom, they felt sorry for him. But from the start, Laura wasn't like that. And although at first he had written her arguments off as silly or naive, some of the things she'd just said were hard not to agree with. Maybe the reason his screenplay ideas were lousy *was* because he was trying too hard for something sufficiently depressing.

Across the cafeteria Mark caught sight of Amanda sitting with a few of her friends. Now there was a girl who wouldn't push him to think too hard about anything . . . except for the kind of thoughts that never bothered him at all.

TWELVE

"I JUST LOVE your room," Amanda cooed on Friday night. "You're really into movies, aren't you?"

The future Rhodes scholar had just deduced that Mark liked movies from the fact that his walls were plastered with movie posters and his bookshelf was crammed with screenplays. Oh, yeah, she was headed for greatness.

Cut her some slack, Mark told himself. "Yeah. I want to go into film," Mark answered.

"Cool!" Amanda squealed in an annoyingly high pitch.

Why was he feeling so irritated with her? Amanda definitely looked great tonight. She was wearing a very short, very tight skirt, with a top that looked more like lingerie than a blouse. But the minute she opened her mouth, he lost all interest. Amanda was the opposite of Laura, who was

135

even more beautiful when she talked. Mark remembered the way her hazel eyes lit up when she got carried away with an idea, the way her smile made him feel so . . . comfortable.

"So, that's why you're directing the play, huh?" Amanda sat down on his bed. She crossed her legs, drawing his eyes to them. Okay, so they weren't as incredible as Laura's, but—

Stop comparing her to Laura! Mark yelled inwardly. *It's pointless. She can't live up to that.*

The problem was, Mark couldn't think of any girl he knew who was as beautiful as Laura Whitman. What was the matter with him? Why was he so obsessed with one girl when there were plenty of others out there? There was even one right in front of him!

"Why don't you sit down?" Amanda asked impatiently, gesturing to the spot next to her. He'd been keeping her occupied for the past half hour with looking around his room, but apparently she was ready to move on.

Moving on is at the top of your to-do list as well, Mark reminded himself. He smiled and sat down beside Amanda, his body almost touching hers. Here was the perfect opportunity to get back into the game, as Doug had suggested. His mom was at her job, so he and Amanda had the apartment to themselves.

Without another word, Mark leaned over to kiss Amanda. She returned the kiss, reaching up to put her arms around his neck. It was perfect—just harmless fun, nothing intense. Exactly what he needed.

Except it was all wrong.

The minute Mark closed his eyes, all he could think of was Laura. Kissing Laura had felt so right, but kissing Amanda seemed forced, unpleasant.

I can't do this. The thought appeared in Mark's head, surprising him. But he knew right then for certain that the last thing he wanted was brainless fun with Amanda. Sure, she was hot—a month ago he could have had a great time with her. But not now. Not tonight.

He pulled away.

Amanda lifted one perfectly plucked eyebrow. "Mark, is something wrong?"

Mark jumped up and crossed over to his desk chair, dropping down onto it. He looked down at the carpet, avoiding Amanda's gaze. "Actually, I'm not feeling that great," he told her. "Maybe we should call it a night."

"What?"

Mark didn't have to look at her face to read her reaction—he could hear it in her voice. The girl was definitely mad. "I just don't feel well, Amanda."

Amanda walked over and stood right before him, forcing him to look at her. Yup, she was *not* happy. "What's your problem?" she asked. "Why did you bring me all the way here for . . . *this?*"

Mark shook his head—he was asking himself the same questions.

"Come on, I'll drive you home," he said.

She looked like she was about to blow. Amanda London probably wasn't used to getting turned down.

"If you take me home now," Amanda said slowly, her mouth a tight line, "do not expect to get another chance."

"All right." Mark shrugged. "Don't forget your jacket," he told her before heading for the door. Then he paused, feeling a little guilty. Amanda might be annoying, but she wasn't a bad person. She didn't deserve to be treated like this. He turned back to face her. "Look, I'm sorry, okay?" he said softly. "This isn't your fault. I think I was just making a mistake here."

Amanda didn't relax her cold glare. "Trust me, you *are* making a mistake," she said. "And don't think you can get out of this by acting like we're friends or something." She reached down and picked up her black jacket from the floor, yanking it on. "Let's just go—now."

Oh, well, I tried, Mark thought as he walked out the door. Now all he could do was follow her instructions and give them both what they wanted—to be far away from each other.

Mark drove up to Mike's house after dropping Amanda off and noticed Doug's Tercel in the driveway. He'd figured both his friends would be there, hanging out in Mike's basement. Mark wished he'd been with them the whole night instead of enduring that torture session with Amanda. She'd been silent until they'd reached her house, and then the only sound she made was the slamming of his car door on her way out.

Now he turned off the ignition and then hopped out of the car, running up to ring the bell. He heard the shuffling of feet inside, then the front door opened.

"Mark, hi! Mike didn't tell me he was expecting you." Mike's mom smiled and stepped back so that he could come inside, closing the door behind him.

"He isn't, actually," Mark told her. "I just kind of showed up. Sorry if I bothered you or interrupted something."

Mrs. Rusignola waved her hand in the air as if to brush off his apology. "You know you're always welcome here," she said. "The guys are downstairs. Do you want anything first, some soda or snacks or anything?"

"No thanks, I'm fine."

"Okay, well, they have chips and stuff down there if you get in the mood. How's everything? How's your mom?"

Mark shifted back and forth, trying to be polite and not reveal how much he didn't feel like making small talk. "Things are good. My mom's working tonight."

Mrs. Rusignola nodded. "She's an incredible woman, your mother."

People said that to Mark a lot. He knew it

was true—his mom *was* amazing for everything she did. But somehow he felt like people just said it because they really didn't know what else to say.

"Yeah, she is," Mark replied, as he always did.

"Well, go on down and have fun with the boys." She gave him one last smile and then walked away, leaving Mark to head for the basement.

When Mark entered the room, he saw that Mike and Doug were playing video games, just as he had expected. They both glanced up and smiled at him.

"Hey!" Doug said. "I thought you were getting hot and heavy with that Amanda chick tonight."

Mark laughed, relieved to be around the two people he could always count on to *not* surprise him. "I wasn't up to it," Mark said with a shrug. He grinned. "Or maybe I was missing you guys too much and had to see how you were surviving without me." He sat down on the floor with them.

"You are such a liar!" Doug shouted. "She shot you down, didn't she?"

Mike smirked. "Yeah. Since when do you choose to play Rampage with us over being with a girl?"

This was *not* a topic he felt like being teased about. "Look, it just wasn't working out, okay? What's the big deal?" Mark asked.

Mike and Doug exchanged looks.

"Finish your game," Mark told them. "I'll take the winner."

Mark sat back and watched his friends as they took turns trying to knock down buildings with a giant gorilla. Then he glanced around at the bowls of chips on the table and the game cartridges lying on the floor. Mike's basement was like a sanctuary from the rest of the world—a place where everything from Mark's mom's health problems to his writer's block stopped mattering and Mark could just goof around with his buddies. At least, that's how he usually felt there. That's what he'd expected to feel tonight. But sitting there, watching Mike and Doug argue over whether it had been the controller's fault or if Doug had really messed up, Mark just felt restless.

"Why don't we turn off the game before you guys kill each other and watch some TV?" Mark suggested.

"Good idea," Doug agreed. "That way I won't have to beat Mike's sorry butt again."

Mike snorted. "Keep dreaming." He switched off the Nintendo and turned on the television.

Mark listened halfheartedly as his friends continued to joke around. But he couldn't help staring off into space rather than focusing on the TV. Was Laura out with Ted at that moment? Where were they? Was she wearing her hair down or up in that braid thing? God, why did he keep thinking about her?

"Okay, Mark, that's it."

"Huh?" Mark looked at Mike distractedly. "What's it?"

Mike's expression darkened, and he glanced at Doug before continuing. "That's exactly what I'm talking about, man. Something's weird with you—you're not acting like yourself."

"And I don't buy the excuses you've been giving me either," Doug chimed in. "So what's the score? What's really going on?"

They were both staring at him, and Mark didn't know what to tell them. "I'm not sure," he said. But he knew that wasn't the truth. He had a very good idea of why he'd turned into the overly sensitive freak from Mars. "Well . . . there *is* something I didn't exactly mention to you guys," he started.

"I knew it!" Doug exclaimed, obviously pleased with himself.

Mike rolled his eyes. "What?" he asked.

"There was this, um—" He paused. "This girl."

"Don't even say it," Doug cut in. "Don't even tell me that a girl has done this to the king of love 'em and leave 'em."

Even Mike looked a little shocked. Did everyone think he was that incapable of caring? Mark wondered.

"It's not like that," Mark assured them. "I mean, it's not like I'm in *love* with her or anything." He felt a strange chill as he said the words but quickly went on. "I just hooked up with her a couple of weeks ago, and I can't seem to get her out of my head."

Mike nodded knowingly, smiling. "You fell for her."

"No, that's not . . ." Mark trailed off, unsure of how to finish.

"So who is she?" Doug asked.

Mark took a deep breath. "Laura Whitman," he said finally. "We hung out at that party I went to."

"So you lied to us?" Mike pretended to look hurt.

"I guess so. But she's a friend of Rosita's, you know? I didn't want to be a jerk about it. Just don't let it get around, okay?"

"Laura Whitman . . . Do we know her?" Doug asked, wrinkling his nose.

"Probably not. She's a junior—she's in the play. Maybe you've seen her around, though. She's tall; dark hair."

Doug shrugged. "I don't know."

"Wait, we're forgetting the important thing here," Mike reminded them. "Mark has got it bad for this girl."

"I don't—I'm not, oh, whatever." Mark gave up. What was he trying to deny? "She's going out with Ted Legum anyway, so it doesn't matter."

"Legum? Man, she's got some bad taste." Mike shook his head. "No offense, Mark. Are they serious?"

"Wait a sec. We're missing the important details

143

here. What do you mean, you hooked up with her?" Doug interjected. "Are we talking pretty intense or the mild stuff?"

"Nothing major," Mark said. "She is an amazing kisser, though." He sighed, remembering how soft her lips were, how she had felt in his arms. God, he *was* turning into a wuss.

"Anyway." He turned back to Mike. "I think she is pretty serious about Ted."

"That stinks," Mike said.

"Okay. What Mark needs right now is to forget about this girl and get over it," Doug advised. "None of us *need* girls. Think about it—we can have a great time, just the three of us here, hanging out and doing our own thing. What could be better?" He gestured at their surroundings. "Naw, man. All girls do is mess with your mind. You really want that? You want to be a slave to some chick?"

Mike laughed, then looked at Mark. "Could he be more of a jerk?"

Mark forced a smile. "It doesn't seem possible." But the truth was, one short month ago he would have agreed with Doug completely.

"I do have to almost agree with the guy, though," Mike said. "I mean, she's already taken, and if she's with someone like Legum, then it doesn't sound like she's really right for you. And face it—you've been a mess lately."

Mark pretended to look offended. "Thanks a lot."

Mike shrugged. "It's true, my man. I think you want this girl, but it doesn't matter if you can't have her. Think about it this way: Why do you need her?"

Yeah, why did he? Mark surveyed the room, taking in all the games, the posters, the Ping-Pong table where he had beat Mike more times than he could remember. Then he looked at his two friends and pictured the way they'd been battling over the video game just a little while ago. How easy it was to spend his weekends here, in Mike's basement with the two of them, goofing around and doing absolutely nothing.

And then it sank in, so clear and so obvious. He *did* need Laura. He loved Mike and Doug—he loved their nights of being stupid together and the way they could take his mind off heavier problems. But the only times that he had felt normal in the past few weeks were the times he'd been with Laura, listening as she made him see things in totally new ways or watching the way she reacted to his stories like they meant something to her. Every time they had talked—about themselves, their lives, or life in general—he'd felt his whole mind expanding, and nothing was what he'd always thought anymore. She'd surprised him over and over with how much more there was to her than he'd originally thought, how much more there was to her than to *anyone* he'd ever known.

The truth was, everything and everyone else

had been boring him or filling him with that restless sense of needing more. It was only when Laura was around, looking at him with those incredible hazel eyes, forcing him to think and to feel, that he was totally okay. Sure, he was attracted to her—that had been a given all along. But now he understood that wasn't all, that wasn't everything. He loved her. He was in love with Laura.

Mike and Doug were still staring at him. Was he ready to give up Nintendo? Ping-Pong? Nights of total male slobness?

He was.

"Because I do," he answered slowly. "I do need her."

Now that he'd said it out loud and his friends were blinking back at him, jaws dropped, a rush of thoughts and emotions began to crowd his head.

How could this have happened? How could he have let himself need anyone, much less a girl like Laura? Still, now that he knew what he'd been feeling these past few weeks, it was impossible to deny it.

He stood up, running his hands through his hair. How was he going to handle this? He'd always known that Laura would never go out with someone like him even if Ted *wasn't* in the picture. Rosita had confirmed that by everything she'd told him. But was there any chance they were wrong? Mark pictured Laura's face, the way she looked at him sometimes when they were together. Sometimes it had seemed like she really *did* feel something.

There's only one way to know the truth, Mark told himself grimly, heading for the door and ignoring the sound of his friends calling after him. *I have to tell her how I feel.*

After all, hadn't Laura been the one to tell him to always expect the best?

THIRTEEN

*T*HE NEW DEAL *was a watershed event in American political history.* How many times had she read that sentence? Laura turned the textbook over on its face and flopped back on her bed. She was finding it impossible to concentrate. Every time she'd try to work on something, her thoughts would wander. She'd picture Mark and wonder how his screenplay scene was going. And she'd want to call him and ask, but she'd feel too weird.

It was funny. She could tell him things that she wouldn't say to anyone else, but at the same time she couldn't even call him just to talk without feeling awkward.

Stop thinking about Mark! she ordered herself. She had a big date with Ted later—dinner at a restaurant downtown. Maybe he would even ask her to be his girlfriend tonight. *That's* what she should be thinking about, not Mark Adams.

Laura groaned, sitting up and pulling her history book back onto her lap. *The New Deal was a watershed*— She slammed the book shut. It was no use.

I'll go talk to Julie, Laura thought. It was a good excuse to avoid studying for a little longer, and besides, she wanted to make sure her sister was really pulling herself together like she'd promised she would. Julie had barely spoken to her since the principal called, and Laura hadn't had time to check in with her sister.

She glanced out the window on her way into the hallway. It was gray and cloudy outside. The sky was darker than it should have been that early in the day—it wasn't even three yet. She smiled to herself, thinking how this was probably Mark's favorite kind of weather.

"Jules?" Laura rapped gently on her sister's open door, noticing with satisfaction that Julie's back was to her. She was sitting at her desk, head bent over.

At least she's doing homework, Laura thought. *That's more than I could say right now.* "Hey, Jules," she called to her. Julie didn't look up. *She must be really into whatever she's working on.* Laura walked farther into the room, coming up behind her sister.

"Boo!" she teased.

Julie jumped and spun around in her chair. Her face was covered with tears.

"Oh my God, Julie, what is it?" Laura exclaimed. "What's wrong?"

"I can't do it. I just can't," Julie sobbed. She motioned at the books on her desk. "I get so exhausted, and so upset and frustrated. I just want to go to sleep and make it all go away for a little while. They said it would get better, but it's just not!"

Laura's mouth opened, but she had no idea what to say. She didn't even know what her sister was talking about. Was something seriously wrong with Julie? "Are you getting sick or something?"

Julie shook her head, wiping away some tears. "No. It's not like that. It mostly just makes me want to sleep."

Still baffled, Laura sat down on Julie's bed. "*What* makes you want to sleep?"

Julie sniffled, not meeting Laura's eyes. "I'm so embarrassed," she confessed. "I didn't want you to know about this—I was afraid you'd think I was just acting like a baby."

"God, Julie, will you just tell me what you're talking about?" Laura cried. Fear made her voice sharper than she meant it to be.

"She's talking about her depression," Laura's mom said from the doorway.

Laura turned to her mother, frowning in confusion. "Huh? What does Julie have to be depressed about?"

"I'm not depressed *about* any one thing," Julie said. "It's clinical depression. That's what the doctor said."

"What doctor?" Laura looked at Julie accusingly.

"You didn't tell me you were going to a doctor!"

Mrs. Whitman walked into the room and sat on the bed next to Laura. "Julie didn't want you to worry about her, but I guess we should have told you right up front," she said with a sigh. "Julie was having some problems at school, and when she told me how she was feeling, I took her to see a psychiatrist."

Laura's mouth dropped open. "You made *me* promise not to tell them about school!" she said to Julie.

"I know, but it just got worse," her sister said tearfully. "One day I couldn't take it anymore—just getting myself on the school bus home was a huge ordeal. I was scared, so I told Mom."

"I don't understand any of this," Laura said.

"When I was . . ." Her mom paused, clearing her throat. "When I was younger, I had this problem. I would go through periods of being very, very depressed. I just felt tired a lot, and I had no appetite or energy. Eventually I was diagnosed with clinical depression. And I know it can be hereditary. But I got help—with therapy and medication I was fine."

Laura sat there in shock. How could her mother have kept something like this from her? A problem that she knew one of her daughters could have, and she hadn't warned them?

"I should have explained all of this a long time ago," Mrs. Whitman continued, as if anticipating Laura's next question. "But a lot of people don't believe depression really exists. They think it's all in your head. You can have this amazing job and an incredible husband and still feel like you never want to get out of bed. And that just doesn't make sense to people who've never felt it."

"But why couldn't you tell *us?*" Laura interrupted.

Her mom's eyes teared up again. "I was afraid if you knew, you'd be embarrassed about me or worried all the time. But once Julie told me how *she* was feeling, I knew we had to get help for her."

Guilt built up in Laura as she remembered how she'd snapped at her sister for not being able to control her moods. According to what their mom was saying, Julie hadn't been able to change anything.

"Well, if nothing is wrong, why do you feel depressed?" Laura asked, trying not to show how upset she was.

"It's a chemical thing," her mother explained. "In some people the chemicals in our brains get messed up and we can't control feeling really down even when nothing's wrong. If you don't get help, it's torture. Your father and I almost separated once before I was able to face that something was wrong and got treatment. *But,*" she stressed, "once I found a doctor who could help, I was okay. And you will be too, Julie, I promise. You just have to give it some more time."

Laura's mind was reeling. Her parents had almost *split up?* What else had happened that they hadn't told her about? Suddenly she felt furious at her mother for keeping this hidden for all these years. And they'd been taking Julie to a psychiatrist, and they hadn't even told her?

A million emotions crowded in Laura. *I need to get out of here,* she thought, her throat tight. If she stayed much longer, she'd freak out in front of Julie. That was not something her sister needed to see right now.

She got up. "I'm sorry, I just need to be alone for a minute, okay?"

"Laura, honey . . ." Her mother looked at her pleadingly.

"Mom, please?"

Mrs. Whitman paused, then nodded.

Laura ran for her bedroom. She shut the door behind her, trying to steady herself. The cordless phone was lying on her floor, and she grabbed it and quickly punched in Rosita's phone number. Nobody answered. Laura hung up on their answering machine.

Who else could she call? There was Ted. Wasn't that the point of having a boyfriend—someone who would be there for her when she really needed him? She dialed his number, letting out her breath when he answered.

"Hi, Ted, it's Laura." She sat down on the floor, pulling her knees into her chest and fighting to keep her voice even.

"Hey, Laura, what's up? Is there a problem with tonight?"

"No, not exactly. I, um, well, I needed to talk to

you about something. It's about my sister."

"Your sister?" Ted sounded puzzled.

"Yes. I haven't said anything about this to you before, but she's been going through a rough time lately."

"Uh-huh."

Ted clearly didn't know where she was going, and the idea of explaining it all to him suddenly seemed overwhelming. Laura let out another deep breath "Well, I just found out that she has this depression thing. I mean, not just being upset for a little while, but some kind of actual depression where she can't do her schoolwork and she's always supertired." Laura bit her lip. This wasn't coming out right. "And my mom just told me that she had it too, but she never said anything about it before. So, you know, I'm worried about Julie, and I can't understand why my mom kept something like that from me." Laura felt tears gathering in her eyes.

Ted was quiet, then seemed to realize she was waiting for a response. "God, that really bites," he said.

That really bites? Getting a D on a test bites. But finding out your parents have kept things from you and your sister is sick? Laura got a cold feeling in her stomach.

"Maybe dinner tonight will cheer you up," he said. "I hear they've got delicious—"

"You know what?" Laura interrupted. "I think I'd rather skip dinner, actually."

"Why? Because of this thing with your sister?"

Laura frowned. "Yeah, Ted. I'm really not into making small talk tonight." She knew she sounded rude, but she didn't care.

"Uh, okay." Ted's tone had cooled. "I guess I'll talk to you later."

"Yeah, whatever," she said. "Bye."

She didn't even wait for him to reply before clicking off the phone. Somewhere inside her Laura realized that the relationship she'd been building up in her head for weeks had just been lost in a matter of minutes. And there was no getting out of facing him as Samantha in *Only Today*. But she couldn't let herself get upset about that—not now, not with everything her sister was going through.

Ted had been right about one thing—getting out of her house would definitely help. She needed air. But Rosita wasn't home.

Mark. He had turned into a good friend despite any weirdness between them. And he, out of everyone, should understand what she was going through since he was always talking about the *misery* in life.

Mark answered after one ring.

"Hi, it's Laura." She barely trusted herself to talk right now without bursting into tears.

"Oh . . . hey." His voice sounded funny, almost nervous. "Is something wrong?"

He could tell that from three words?

"Yeah, actually. Something is really wrong. I— look, I don't really want to talk over the phone.

Actually, I kind of need to get out of here. Is there any way you could come pick me up?"

"I'll be right there." Laura hung up and bit her lip. All she had to do was hold on until Mark got here, and then everything would be okay. At least, more okay than it was right now.

She peeked into her sister's room, relieved to see that Julie and her mom were still deep in conversation and Julie looked much calmer. She would talk to Julie later—just the two of them. But first she had to get herself in good enough shape to be able to help her sister. Right now, she was barely in control of her *own* emotions.

Laura went downstairs and watched out the living-room window anxiously, waiting to see Mark's car drive up. Every minute of being in that house was making her feel worse.

She looked at the heavy, dark clouds that were blocking the sun completely. Weather like this had always seemed ominous to Laura—as if the sky was getting ready for something horrible. When the rain finally came, she always felt a little relieved, like, Okay, this is the worst, and it's not that bad. *But I didn't have any warnings of how bad today would be,* Laura thought.

She finally spotted Mark's old car. "I'm going out," she yelled as she headed out the front door, not even stopping for a jacket. Laura jumped into the passenger seat before Mark had a chance to get out.

He looked at her in surprise, raising his eyebrows.

"Can we just go?" she asked.

He nodded and backed out of her driveway onto the road. After they'd made it a few blocks from her house, he finally spoke. "Is there somewhere you wanted to go?"

"I, um, I hadn't really thought about it," she replied, blinking back tears.

"How about Riverview Park? It's kind of cool looking outside right now."

Laura smiled despite herself. She'd known Mark would like this kind of weather. "That's fine," she answered.

They drove the rest of the way in silence. Laura wasn't quite ready to talk about everything, and she figured Mark was respecting that.

Mark pulled up to the side of the park, and they stepped out of the car, walking over to a bench in front of the river. Nobody else was around, to Laura's relief. She knew she wouldn't be able to hold in her emotions much longer, and she couldn't deal with an audience. But somehow Mark seeing her like this was okay. She didn't know why. It just was.

"Hey, you must be kind of chilly," Mark said after they sat down. "I'm sorry, I wasn't even thinking—you're not dressed for this weather." The wind was whipping the air around her, blowing in her face and sending ripples of water across the river. But she hadn't even realized she felt cold.

"No, I'm fine," she protested, glancing at her jeans and thin, white T-shirt. "I like it out here."

And she did. The coldness on her face seemed like a layer of protection from what was going on in her head.

"Put this on," Mark insisted, pulling his windbreaker over his head and handing it to her.

Laura slipped the dark blue jacket on over her shirt.

"So, do you want to tell me what's going on?" he prodded gently. "Why did you suddenly have to get away from a family you're always singing the praises of?"

Laura winced, remembering how she'd told Mark over and over how her parents were proof that families could be perfect. *He was right about everything,* she thought. *He was right, and I was wrong.*

"I should have listened to you," she blurted out. "My family's a mess. Everything's a mess, and I feel so stupid."

Mark watched her closely, his expression surprised but compassionate. He moved toward her. "What happened?"

Laura sighed. "You know how my sister, Julie, has been sleeping, like, all the time lately?"

Mark nodded. "She was taking a nap the day I came over."

"Yeah, well, basically she was taking one *every* day. And she's been acting weird too. I don't know, she's just seemed . . . not really interested in life. And then the principal called, and it turned out that she hadn't been going to all her classes or

159

doing her work." Laura stopped. Telling all this to Mark now, it seemed so obvious that something had been really wrong with Julie. Why hadn't Laura taken it more seriously? "I failed her," she continued softly. "I was the one who knew her best. I could tell she wasn't acting normal, and I didn't help her."

"What's wrong with her?"

"She has depression. I mean, *real* depression, some kind of chemical thing. She can't control being really tired and worn out all the time or the problems she has with focusing on things."

"Yeah, I know what clinical depression is," Mark said. "It can get pretty awful." He paused. "But Laura, you shouldn't be this upset about it. I mean, at least Julie doesn't have anything life threatening, right? They have medication that helps depression."

"You're right." She took a deep breath, hugging herself. "But mostly I'm just so mad at my mom. She explained all of this today—about depression, what it is and everything. And the reason she knew so much was because she has it too!"

"Really? Your mom?" Mark asked.

Laura nodded. "But she never told us! She knew it could be passed down genetically, but she never even warned us. Here I was, thinking my family was the greatest because there were no secrets, but my parents were keeping a huge one all along. They didn't even tell me they were taking Julie to a psychiatrist! Can you believe it?" Mark opened his mouth to respond, but Laura went on. "I know, *you're* not surprised at all. You're the one who told me that every silver lining has a giant cloud covering it. Well, you were right."

Mark ran a hand through his hair. "Laura, I'm sorry about all of this. And I'm sorry if I made you think that I would—" He turned away, staring at the river for a second, then met her eyes again. His eyes reflected a mixture of pain and confusion, like a mirror of what she felt inside. "I was wrong to tell you that nothing could ever work out. I mean, I understand why this is hard for you. Really, really hard. But I don't think it's as terrible as you see it."

Laura felt her temper flare. Was he just going to be like Ted and brush this off? She had thought Mark would be the one person who would understand why this hurt so much. He knew what it was like to worry about someone he loved. How could he not get this?

As soon as Mark saw the look on her face, he reached out and grabbed her shoulder. "No, I didn't mean that how it sounded," he said firmly. "Knowing Julie is in pain has got to be devastating for you." Laura gulped, nodding. "And to find out at the same time that your mom kept something from you is a double blow. You trusted her completely, and now you're doubting her, even doubting yourself." Laura's eyes widened. It was like Mark was describing her feelings better than even she could. "But did she say why she never told you?" he asked.

"Yes," Laura answered, kicking at the dirt with her foot. "She said it was for us—so that we wouldn't have to worry all the time or be ashamed of her or something crazy like that."

Mark sighed, dropping his hand from Laura's shoulder. She shivered, suddenly feeling the cold sharply.

"Mothers don't tell you stuff when they think it will upset you. My mom lies all the time when she pretends she's okay, even though I can tell her back is killing her. It's frustrating, but I know that it only means she loves me so much that she wants to protect me. Which is more than I can say for my dad."

Laura glanced at the river, watching the water get tossed by the wind and processing Mark's words. He was right. What her mom had done was nothing compared to abandoning your wife and son.

"So, what are you saying?" she asked quietly, fixing her gaze back on Mark. "You, the king of pessimism, are telling me there's a happy ending in here?"

Mark's mouth turned up in a slight smile. Laura felt warm from the way he looked at her, safe. "Your sister *is* going to be okay. This isn't the end of the world." He shrugged. "Maybe your family isn't exactly what you thought. But you still have two parents and a sister who you love and who love you. This is when you stop, accept that life doesn't have to be perfect, and deal with the big issue—helping Julie get better."

Laura stared at Mark in amazement. Listening to him, things actually made sense to her. Unlike Ted, he understood why she was so upset. He also made her realize that things weren't as bad as she'd thought they were an hour ago. And somehow he'd managed to explain it all by turning her own words around on her!

"So you actually agree with me, then, about life not being one great big tragedy," Laura said, starting to smile.

Mark grinned back. "I wouldn't go that far," he teased. "But I guess I realized that you might have a few good points." He squeezed her arm. "Seriously, Laura, your family is very special. You've made that extremely clear to me in the past. Now you just need to remind yourself."

Laura nodded, tears welling up in her eyes. Suddenly all she wanted was to be back with her family, helping Julie get through this.

"You know what?" she told Mark. "I should go back. I'm sorry, I know you must think I'm psycho today, but they're probably all pretty worried about me now, and I think I should be there. I think—well, I think what you said makes a lot of sense."

Mark smiled for a second, then his face turned serious. "Before we go, I kind of wanted to . . ." He hesitated, then shook his head. "Never mind. You're right—you should get home."

Laura studied him, wondering what he wanted to say. "No, we can wait a minute." She inched closer to him on the bench. Mark had been there

163

for her when she needed it most—she wasn't going to let him down.

He looked at Laura for a long moment, giving her that now familiar nervous feeling, the one where her stomach was churning around inside, but she somehow didn't mind.

Then he suddenly coughed and stood up, reaching out his hand to help her to her feet. "It can wait. Right now you have to be with your family."

Laura grabbed Mark's hand and jumped up next to him. "If you're sure . . . ," she said uncertainly.

"I'm sure. Come on, let's go." Mark turned and started walking.

Laura couldn't wait to find out what he had to say, but Mark was right. Whatever it was could wait. Right now, she had her family to think about.

FOURTEEN

WIMP, COWARD, CHICKEN. Mark racked his brain for every appropriate insult to call himself after his total failure to tell Laura the truth about his feelings. There he was, explaining why her parents had felt the need to keep something from her, and he was holding something giant back from her the whole time.

That's totally different, he rationalized, easing up on the accelerator after noticing that he was speeding down a side road. Her mom had withheld something that could have cleared up a lot of stuff for her and her sister. His news, on the other hand, would just create more stress and confusion for Laura. After all, he knew she didn't feel the same way. He knew she was happy with Ted.

For some reason, Mark went straight through the intersection where he should have turned right to get to his house. Apparently going home wasn't what he wanted right now.

What I really want is to be with Laura, hearing her laugh and looking into those killer eyes of hers. But that wasn't possible. At least, not this instant. So he started to drive back toward Riverview Park.

Truthfully, the reason he'd finally held back from confessing to Laura was that it wouldn't have been fair to her to pile his revelation on top of what she'd already been trying to deal with.

Wait, Mark thought suddenly, *why did Laura come to me with everything anyway?* Mark reached the park, and he swung into the spot he'd been in earlier. Until now, he hadn't even questioned the fact that when Princess Laura had encountered her first serious crisis, she had called *him,* not her Ted in shining armor. So, then she had to trust him— and feel something for him—to go to him about such a personal problem, right?

Maybe Ted wasn't home. Maybe he was out getting a pedicure or whatever guys like him do to stay pretty. But still, even if Ted had been busy, Laura had turned to Mark like it was the natural thing to do. Any *YM* advice columnist would agree that there was significance there.

And he was so glad that she had come to him, so relieved that he'd been able to make things better for her. Seeing Laura like that, so upset, had been hard. Harder than he ever would have imagined. *Of course, I never imagined I would fall for anyone like this either.* He was supposed to be immune to mushy lovesickness, allergic to affection. Yeah, right. He was as bad as the worst of them right now, torturing himself over whether or not to admit to Laura that he was completely, utterly, head-over-clichéd heels in love with her.

Mark turned off the engine and stepped out of his car, pacing anxiously around the park. He stared at the bench where they had been sitting not long ago, remembering how badly he'd wanted to hold her.

This was ridiculous. He had to talk to her—he couldn't keep this inside a moment longer. One thing Laura had taught him was that nothing was as certain as you thought, and people could always surprise you.

He jogged back to the car and started it up, heading back in the direction of Laura's house. He was about to make her words a reality.

"I'm so glad you're all right," Mrs. Whitman told Laura. The whole family was gathered in the living room, talking. When Laura had walked into her house a short while earlier, her parents had been sitting on the couch with Julie. Her dad had immediately jumped up and hugged her, pulling her over to join them. No one was mad at her for leaving—they had just been worried about where she'd gone and if she was okay.

Now Laura looked down at her feet. "I am. I just can't believe you kept this from me." She glanced back up at her mom. "And I'm still really confused about why you did," she continued. "But I was with my friend Mark, and he helped me see what matters." She reached over to take Julie's hand. "All I want is for Julie to get better and for us to do it as a family, like always."

"Thanks," Julie said quietly. "I know I'll feel better after I'm on my medicine for a while. It's just frustrating sometimes."

"I'm sorry you're so hurt by this too, Laura," Mr. Whitman said. "From now on we all come to each other about *everything*, okay?"

They all nodded.

"Well," her mom said, "I'm glad it's all out in the open now, Laura. I'm relieved that you aren't more upset with me for keeping this from you."

"You can thank Mark for that," Laura said. "After talking to him, it didn't seem like it made any sense to be mad." That was the truth—Mark had been amazing, saying all the things that helped the most.

"I don't know too much about this Mark guy," her dad began, "but I'm glad he was there for you."

Mark. Mark *had* been there for her. Wasn't that what she always said her ideal boyfriend would do?

Laura froze. Mark? But he was the total opposite of what she was looking for, right?

Images of her and Mark together over the past few weeks rushed to her brain. She tried to sort through them. Ever since that night at the party she'd been brushing off her attraction to him. But the pull he'd had on her went way beyond the fact that he was such a good kisser. She felt *right* with him. Even if they didn't think in identical ways, she enjoyed their arguments much more than her small talk with Ted. Mark always made her think about everything and see issues from new angles. And today, when she'd really needed him, he'd showed her how to look at something important in a different way, making the scariest thing that had ever happened to her seem bearable. Wasn't all of that what really mattered when it came down to it? Had Ted's reliability done any good when she'd needed someone to listen, care, and understand?

Oh my God, Laura realized, shocked. *I've been ignoring the most completely obvious thing in the world!* She was in love with Mark.

What was she going to do? What if he laughed at her? What if he started to avoid her, the way he avoided all the other girls who thought they were special to him?

It doesn't matter, she thought. *I still have to tell him the truth. If we're really right for each other, I have to know. And if he laughs at me, well . . . I'll find a way to deal with that, just like I'll find a way to deal with Julie's illness.*

Laura looked at her family. She didn't want to leave them again like this, in the middle of such a crisis. But suddenly she needed to talk to Mark more than she'd ever needed to do anything.

"Um, is everyone . . . I mean, are we okay?"

Her mom cocked her head. "What is it? Is something else bothering you?"

"It's just that—well, I'm fine, but there's . . . something I need to do right now." Her parents exchanged puzzled looks.

Before they could answer, the doorbell rang. Mr. Whitman went to answer it, and Laura glanced over to see who was there.

Mark.

Her heart seemed to stop beating and to race even faster at the same time. She couldn't believe it—it was like he had magically appeared *again* when she needed him most. But why had he come?

He was standing on her front steps, his hair a total mess from the wind. He glanced around at her family. "I'm—uh, I'm sorry. I should go, I guess." He turned around.

"No! Mark, wait." Laura ran over to him. She looked back at her parents. "I just have to talk to him for a little while. I'll be back soon, okay?" *Please don't say no, please don't say no.*

"Go ahead, Laura," her dad told her. "We'll finish talking when you get back."

"Thanks, Dad." Laura gave him a quick squeeze, then rushed outside, shutting the door behind her.

She faced Mark, and they both stood there for a moment, saying nothing. But somehow their silence felt more meaningful than any words she and Ted had ever exchanged. Then they started walking down her block, side by side.

"Hey, it's finally starting to rain," Laura said when they'd reached the corner. The drops were coming down lightly, and it felt good, refreshing.

"Yeah." Mark looked up at the sky, then back at her. "Laura, there's something I have to tell you."

"No, wait, let me go first." She knew if she didn't get it out right away, she'd lose her courage completely.

"What I have to say is more important," Mark said firmly. "I know it's pointless for me to even tell you this and that you're happy with Ted, and I know this is terrible timing and you should be with your family." He paused. "I'm talking like you," he said, smiling. The rain started to fall harder. "Laura, I love you," he blurted out. "I'm in love with you. I thought about how to tell you, and I couldn't figure out anything that wouldn't sound stupid. This is nothing like me—I've never been like this, and I don't know how to . . . I don't know what I'm doing. But I love you, and I had to tell you."

He stared at her expectantly. Laura looked back into his amazing blue eyes, too stunned to speak. This moment was everything she'd ever dreamed of, but better. Now she felt a true sense of security—the security of being loved by the person who made her melt inside.

Mark's face fell when she didn't respond right away. "I knew it," he started. "I'm sorry, I knew you would never see me as more than a friend. I *knew* I didn't fit into your life. I—"

Laura burst out laughing, grabbing Mark and

pulling herself to him. His jacket was soaked, but she clasped his back tightly. "Mark—shut up!" she yelled. "I am so in love with you, I came out here to tell you the same thing!"

He started to smile—a huge, silly grin that covered his face. "Really?" he asked. "What about Ted?"

Laura shook her head, smiling back at Mark. "Ted was a mistake," she said. "And I can't believe it took me this long to see it. But I was so sure you didn't want to be with me."

He reached out and held her face in his hands, the water from his fingers dripping onto her already wet skin. "I've wanted nothing else ever since I kissed you," he told her, his voice thick with emotion. "Only I was busy being just as blind to it as you were."

"Let's make a deal," Laura said, looking right into his eyes. "Let's never ignore what's right in front of us again, okay?"

"I promise," Mark said. And then he leaned down to kiss her, his lips meeting hers in the softest, most passionate, heart-stopping kiss she had ever imagined. The rain surrounded them, beating down on them, but all Laura could feel was Mark's mouth on hers and his arms around her.

And the sensation of floating on clouds made of cotton candy.

EPILOGUE

"YOU GUYS RULE," Rosita said to Mark, flinging her arms around his neck. "This is the coolest surprise ever! You and Laura make a good team. Obviously." She pulled back and smiled, her eyes sparkling. It was Saturday night, and Rosita's birthday party was in full swing.

"You knew this would happen all along, didn't you?" Mark asked.

"Oh, yeah," Rosi told him. "I just had to let you guys figure it out on your own. Dennis is probably pretty mad he's missing all the fun," she added, her smile dimming a tiny bit.

"Well, he should be calling any minute to say happy birthday," Mark told her. "He knew all about the party. And speaking of missing people, have you seen your best friend around? I've been looking for her." Mark scanned the living room. So far he hadn't gotten any alone time with Laura tonight.

"Since when does a girl have you whipped like this?" Rosita teased him.

"I am not whipped," Mark argued. "I'm . . . pureed, maybe. And none of this gives you the right to make fun of me," he told her. But it was pointless. Ever since the last party he'd been to with Laura Whitman, he'd lost all chances of remaining a proudly bitter guy.

He'd never been so happy to lose anything in his life.

Laura was in the kitchen, getting the birthday cake ready, when Mark walked in. "Where have you been all night?" she asked him, carefully placing the candles in the chocolate icing.

"I was about to ask you the same thing," he told her, coming up behind her and putting his arms around her waist. "So, guess what?"

"What?"

"I finished my screenplay scene today."

"That's great! What did you end up writing about?" Laura turned back to the cake, finishing the decorations.

"I wrote about this guy and this girl who both learn that their worlds aren't exactly what they thought, and they help each other figure out what's true and what isn't. And then they fall in love."

Laura dropped the candles, spinning around to look at him.

"You inspired it, Laura, the whole thing," he

said. "I just sat down and wrote, and it all came out so easily."

"I inspired you?" Laura reached out to touch his cheek. "What happens to the characters in the end?"

Mark kissed her—a deep, long kiss. She felt the familiar mix of excitement and contentment surge through her body. Then he pulled back a little, his face still inches away from hers.

"Is this a happy enough ending for you?" he asked.

Laura laughed. "Yes," she answered. "This works perfectly."

Do you ever wonder about falling in love? About members of the opposite sex? Do you need a little friendly advice but have no one to turn to? Well, that's where we come in . . . Jenny and Jake. Send us those questions you're dying to ask, and we'll give you the straight scoop on life and love.

DEAR JAKE

Q: *I'm dating two guys who—fortunately—live in different cities. Although it's not likely that one will find out about the other, I wonder if what I'm doing is right. I kind of feel like I'm cheating even though I don't have a commitment with either one. Since I'm fairly new at dating, I'm not too sure what the rules are. Is it okay to continue seeing both of them, or do I have to choose?*

JY, Portland, OR

A: Why should you have to choose? You say that there's no commitment with either of these guys. If that's the case—and they're both aware of it—there's no need to stop seeing one of them. As for the rules, the only ones that I'm aware of have to do with honesty and communication. Make sure you're clear with both of these guys about the whole "not exclusive" thing so there are no misunderstandings. You don't want to give either one the wrong impression—that could cause confusion and hurt feelings. If both of these guys understand that you're not looking for a serious relationship right now, then have fun with it!

Q: *I broke up with my boyfriend, Bryan, about six months ago, and I am totally over him. But he just started dating my younger sister's best friend, Katherine. (She's two years younger than me.) It's so weird because they both know so much about me. I feel like they're comparing notes, and it makes me uncomfortable around them. What can I do?*

KH, Durham, NC

A: The good news is, Katherine is your sister's friend, not yours. I'm guessing that means you don't have to be around them all the time. You're probably just bumping into the couple every once in a while, and I'm sure you can handle that gracefully.

The other good news (I'm just full of good news!) is that I sincerely doubt Katherine and Bryan are comparing notes about you. If Bryan is a good guy, he's not going to go blabbing about things you might have told him or done with him. Not only would that hurt you, but I'm sure he knows talking about an ex-girlfriend with a new girlfriend is not cool. And I'm sure Katherine isn't bringing you up either. Do you really think she wants to set herself up for comparison to your perfect self? Doubtful. So stop stressing, and concentrate on your own happiness.

DEAR JENNY

Q: *I'm fifteen, and I've had a crush on a guy in my class all year. Last week he finally asked me out. The problem is that he's Latino and I'm white. I'm pretty sure my parents would never let me date him, but I really like this guy a lot, and I don't believe that race should make a difference. I'm torn between going out with him and not telling my parents and turning him down without an explanation. What should I do?*

HP, Wapakoneta, OH

A: I'm sure it's frustrating being in this position, especially if you really like the guy. But I wouldn't advise sneaking around behind your parents' backs. That always leads to trouble. You said your parents would never let you date him, but have you discussed this with them? If you haven't, that's the first thing you need to do. It's possible that your parents might surprise you. Be honest with them—tell them how you feel and make sure you point out all of the reasons why this is important to you. Why don't you suggest they meet him before making a decision? Hopefully they'll be impressed with your maturity and openness—and with your crush! If, however, they don't go for it, you can still be friends with this guy, and your friendship can continue to grow by hanging out with him and your other friends.

Q: *I've had a lot of bad experiences with guys, and I finally decided that I should just stop dating completely. I'm really sick of* getting hurt. My friend told me that I'm being silly and that the best thing to do is to keep dating until I find the right guy. Is she right?

EA, Philadelphia, PA

A: You've been burned pretty badly, so you need to take a break and heal a little. There's nothing silly about that—in fact, it's quite healthy of you to watch out for yourself. When you jump from one bad relationship to another without taking a time-out, you lose your perspective and judgment in the rush.

But there's another issue here that your friend seems to have picked up on. You've decided that the unpleasant experiences you've had with guys mean that every guy and every relationship will lead to pain for you. Declaring that you will never date again is a pretty serious statement. I can't tell you that you'll never get hurt again because there's a chance you might. But when you take that risk, you're also opening yourself up to all of the thrill, excitement, and joy of love. And—trust me—that's something you don't want to miss out on.

Q: *John is the first and only guy I've ever been in love with. We've been together for almost four years! Last week I found out that my family is moving to New York, all the way across the country. What should I do? Everybody keeps telling me we should just break up. But I love him, and the thought of losing him tears me apart.*

SS, Seattle, WA

A: I can't tell you whether or not to break things off with John when you move since ultimately the only person who knows what feels right is you. But I can give you a few hints on how to make this huge decision.

Keep in mind that you are going to a completely new place, where you will be forging new friendships and finding a way to fit in. Knowing that there is someone supporting you from afar could give you strength, but it could also hold you back from throwing yourself fully into your new life. When you're pining for someone thousands of miles away, it's hard to get too attached to the things that are right there in front of you.

None of this matters, though, if you remain convinced that your bond with John can withstand any amount of distance and if this in fact proves true. Once you move, you'll be able to see how your and John's relationship is affected. If the only thing that makes sense to you is staying together——and neither of you are having serious adjustment problems in the rest of your lives——then there's no reason to break up.

Do you have questions about love? Write to:
Jenny Burgess or Jake Korman
c/o 17th Street Productions,
a division of Daniel Weiss Associates, Inc.
33 West 17th Street
New York, NY 10011

Don't miss any of the books in *Love Stories*
—the romantic series from Bantam Books!

Super Editions

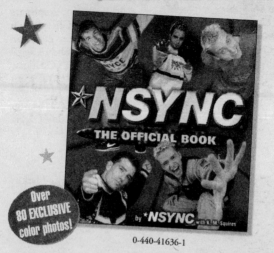

You'll always remember your first love.

Looking for signs he's ready to fall in love?

Want the guy's point of view?

Then you should check out *Love Stories*. Romantic stories that tell it like it is—why he doesn't call, how to ask him out, when to say good-bye.

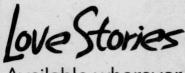
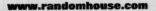